Tanigawa, Nagaru.
The indignation of
Haruhi Suzumiya /
2012.
33305225929938
sa          02/13/13

D0338138

# THE INDIGNATION
## OF HARUHI SUZUMIYA

# NAGARU TANIGAWA

**LITTLE, BROWN AND COMPANY**
NEW YORK  BOSTON

Yen
Press

This book is a work of fiction. Names, characters, places, and incidents
are the product of the author's imagination or are used fictitiously.
Any resemblance to actual events, locales, or persons, living or dead, is
coincidental.

Suzumiya Haruhi No Fungai copyright © Nagaru TANIGAWA 2006
Illustration by Noizi Ito

First published in Japan in 2006 by Kadokawa Shoten Co., LTD., Tokyo.
English hardcover/paperback translation rights arranged with Kadokawa
Shoten Co., LTD., Tokyo, through Tuttle-Mori Agency, Inc., Tokyo.

English translation by Paul Starr

English translation copyright © 2012 by Hachette Book Group, Inc.

All rights reserved. In accordance with the U.S. Copyright Act of 1976,
the scanning, uploading, and electronic sharing of any part of this book
without the permission of the publisher is unlawful piracy and theft of
the author's intellectual property. If you would like to use material from
the book (other than for review purposes), prior written permission
must be obtained by contacting the publisher at permissions@hbgusa.com.
Thank you for your support of the author's rights.

Little, Brown and Company

Hachette Book Group
237 Park Avenue, New York, NY 10017
Visit our website at www.lb-teens.com
www.jointhesosbrigade.com

Little, Brown and Company is a division of Hachette Book Group, Inc.
The Little, Brown name and logo are trademarks of Hachette Book
Group, Inc.

First U.S. Edition: November 2012

Library of Congress Cataloging-in-Publication Data

Tanigawa, Nagaru.
[Suzumiya Haruhi no fungai. English]
The indignation of Haruhi Suzumiya / Nagaru Tanigawa.
p. cm.
Summary: In the first of two stories, a new student council president
threatens to disband the SOS Brigade, a supernatural club posing as a
literature club, and in the second, Haruhi suspects that the neighborhood
dogs are being haunted by animal spirits.
ISBN 978-0-316-03900-0 (hardcover)—ISBN 978-0-316-03899-7 (pbk.)
[1. Supernatural—Fiction.   2. Clubs—Fiction.   3. High schools—Fiction
4. Schools—Fiction   5. Japan—Fiction.]   I. Title.
PZ7.T16139Ind 2012
[Fic]—dc23
2012013848

10 9 8 7 6 5 4 3 2 1

RRD-C

Printed in the United States of America

# THE
## OF HARUHI SUZUMIYA
# INDIGNATION

NAGARU TANIGAWA

First released in Japan in 2003, *The Melancholy of Haruhi Suzumiya* quickly established itself as a publishing phenomenon, drawing much of its inspiration from Japanese pop culture and Japanese comics in particular. With this foundation, the original publication of each book in the Haruhi series included several black-and-white spot illustrations as well as a four-page color insert—all of which are faithfully reproduced here to preserve the authenticity of the first-ever English edition.

# EDITOR IN CHIEF, FULL SPEED AHEAD!

"No good," said Haruhi flatly, thrusting the manuscript back.

"It's not good enough?" whined Asahina. "But I thought about it really hard…"

"Yeah, no way. Not even close. It's got no punch." Haruhi leaned back in the chair at her brigade chief's desk and grabbed the red pen she'd stuck behind her ear. "Just for starters, this introduction is such a cliché. 'Once upon a time'? It's got no freshness to it at all. It needs a twist. The intro has to be super catchy, got it? First impressions are critical."

"But," said Asahina tremulously, "that's how fairy tales are supposed to start…"

"That thinking is obsolete!" Haruhi's rejection was haughty and total. "You need to transform your approach. If you think you might have heard something before, then do the opposite. That's the way to bring something new to life."

I got the feeling that the reason it felt like we were leaving the original point of all this activity far behind was thanks to the system Haruhi had just described. It certainly wasn't like the threatening feint of a pitcher who's trying to hold a fast runner at first base, but just doing the opposite wasn't going to work either.

"Anyway, this is no good." Haruhi deliberately wrote "rewrite" with her red pen on the copy-paper manuscript, then tossed it into a cardboard box beside the desk. In the box (which formerly had contained oranges) was a mountain of papers she'd decided was bound for the incinerator. "Write something new."

"Ugh..."

Shoulders slumping, Asahina made her way back to her own seat. She looked truly pathetic. I felt violently sympathetic to her as she picked up a pencil, then held her head in her hands.

I cast my gaze over to a corner of the table from which emanated nothing at all, and there was that most important fixture for the clubroom: Nagato, who was not reading.

"..."

She stared at the display of the laptop computer in front of her, stock-still, typing something on the keyboard every few seconds, whereupon she would turn inanimate yet again.

Nagato was using the laptop we'd won in our battle against the computer club. Similar machines were in front of both Koizumi and myself, their CPU cooling fans spinning away despite the CPUs themselves not really having anything to think about. Koizumi's fingers typed away deftly, the sound of each keystroke grating on my nerves. How nice for him, that he'd decided what he was going to write about.

Asahina, the only one of us to express a prejudice against using machines, was writing by hand on a sheet of copy paper, but she'd stopped, as though synchronized with me.

Of course I'd stopped. How was I supposed to type with nothing to write?

"That goes for everybody else too!" Haruhi alone was strangely energetic. "If you don't hurry to hand in those manuscripts and get the editing done, you won't make it in time for publication. Time to shift into high gear! Just think a little harder and you'll

be able to write something. It's not like we're writing epics or aiming for literary prizes here."

As usual, Haruhi's cheerful face bloomed with that strange energy of hers. Like she was about to devour an insect.

"Kyon, I don't see your hands moving. Sitting there staring at the screen isn't going to get a sentence written. Just write the thing, then print it out and let me take a look at it. If it's good, it passes, and if it's not, then it won't."

My sympathy for Asahina turned into pity for myself. Why did I have to do this, anyway? And it wasn't just me—shouldn't the moaning Asahina beside me and the beatifically smiling Koizumi across from me be raising some kind of flag of mutiny?

All that said, the brigade chief known as Haruhi Suzumiya specialized in not listening to anything anybody said. Still, why had she decided on *this* particular role, of all things?

My gaze moved from Haruhi, who sat there just itching for people to toss their manuscripts into the cardboard box, to the armband wrapped around her arm.

Normally it read "Brigade Chief," though in the past it had also been "Detective" and "Ultra Director." But now a new title was scribbled on the cloth in large Magic-Markered letters.

It was: "Editor in Chief."

This all started a few days earlier.

It was a day in the third term of school as the footsteps of the approaching New Year were starting to become audible. It happened during an otherwise peaceful lunch hour—a bit more warning would've been nice.

"Summons."

It was Yuki Nagato who spoke. For some reason she was accompanied by the ever-composed Itsuki Koizumi. The two of them coming by my classroom together didn't give me so much as a single micron of anything like a good feeling, and although I'd been the one who'd interrupted the business of stirring up my lunch to come into the hallway, I wanted nothing more than to get back to my own desk.

"What do you mean, 'summons'?"

I could only think of my current situation. Taniguchi had been on his way back from buying some pastries and a melon drink when he'd called out, "Hey, Kyon, your cohorts are here," which was why I'd gotten up and was now standing where I was. The particular pairing that confronted me was wholly unlikely, but as far as a suitable partner for Nagato to pair up with went, I couldn't think of a single person I'd approve of.

After looking for about three seconds at the alien girl who stood there after delivering her mysterious "summons," I gave up and regarded Koizumi's handsome face.

"So are you going to explain?"

"Of course, that is why I have come," said Koizumi, craning his neck to look inside Class 5's classroom. "Do you think Suzumiya will be out for a while?"

She'd taken off right after fourth period ended. I figured she was munching away on her lunch in the cafeteria right about now, I said.

"Excellent. This is something I'd rather she not hear."

I got the feeling it was going to be something I'd rather not hear too.

"Actually—" Koizumi lowered his voice.

It seemed like he was enjoying this, I told him.

"Well, whether or not one finds this enjoyable depends on the person."

"Just tell me what it is already."

"We've received a message from the student council president. We're to appear in the student council room today after school. In short, it is a summons."

Ah hah.

I suddenly understood.

"So it's finally come, eh?"

An order to appear in front of the student council president—I wasn't so naive that I couldn't imagine why such a thing would happen. I was too good of a person to ignore the many misdeeds perpetrated by the SOS Brigade both in and out of the school this past year. Had it been the time we'd scammed computers from the computer club? No, wait, we'd settled that in trial by video-game combat the previous autumn. I'd heard that the president of the computer club had withdrawn his complaint with the student council after the loss.

Was it because we'd gone too far when we filmed our movie? That had been a while ago by now, and student council elections had been after the school festival. Had the current council suddenly remembered the business left to them by the previous administration? Or had the physical descriptions of the brigade members that had surely circulated among the neighborhood shrines and temples finally made it to North High? We'd visited a few too many places during our first shrine visit of the New Year, after all.

"Guess there's nothing we can do about it," I said, shrugging and looking back at my unoccupied desk next to the window. "I bet Haruhi'll be thrilled to go mano a mano with the president. Depending on their attitudes, this could turn violent. I'm counting on you for mediation, Koizumi."

"You misunderstand." Koizumi pleasantly refuted me. "It is not Suzumiya who is being summoned."

So, what, it was me? C'mon, that didn't make any sense. It would be the height of injustice if I had to bear the full brunt of the backlash just because Haruhi was as defiant and stubborn as a mule. I knew the student council members were basically the school administration's puppets, but if they were *that* cowardly, I'd be pretty disappointed.

"No, it is not you," said Koizumi, even more pleasantly, like he was happy about something. "It is Nagato alone who has been summoned."

What? That made even less sense. She was great as a target for lecturing, since she'd certainly sit there and silently listen to whatever you said, but I didn't think it'd be very satisfying for the lecturer, since she'd just as certainly stick to her "no comment" policy.

"Nagato?! The student council president wants to see *Nagato*?"

"Your subject and object are both correct. Yes, the president has indicated Nagato."

As for Nagato herself, she simply stood there, as though she had no thoughts of herself at all. She accepted the wave of surprise that emanated from my eyes, her hair fluttering minutely.

"What do you mean? What business does the student council have with Nagato? Don't tell me they want to make her secretary."

I wanted him to just spit it out already. Was his infuriatingly roundabout manner carved into his DNA?

"My apologies. I'll explain it as understandably as I can. The reason Nagato has been summoned is simple: they want to discuss the literature club's activities, particularly in regards to its ongoing existence."

"The literature club? What does—"

*What does that have to do with anything?* I was about to say— but choked back the words.

"..."

Nagato, still unmoving, looked down the hall.

Her pale, once-bespectacled face looked just as it had back then. I would never forget how she looked when Haruhi had burst into her clubroom, dragging me along, and Nagato had looked slowly, expressionlessly up at us.

"I see. The literature club, eh? So that's how it is."

The SOS Brigade's long occupation of the literature club's room for its headquarters was the very embodiment of the present progressive tense. Nagato was the only proper member of the literature club, whereas we were freeloaders at best, and possibly illegal occupants. Haruhi surely felt we'd long since asserted exclusive rights over the space, but the student council was undoubtedly insisting upon a different standard.

Koizumi must have read my facial expression. "They want to talk to the club president about exactly that, face-to-face, after school. The notice came to me first. I passed it on to Nagato."

Why'd it go to him? I wanted to know.

"Perhaps because they knew it would be ignored if they gave it directly to her."

Maybe that was so, but Koizumi and I were just about equivalent in our total lack of association with the literature club, I pointed out.

"That is true, but things aren't necessarily so simple. That may make things even worse. Since we're occupying the literature club's space without doing anything even remotely related to literature, you wouldn't have to be the student council to find that questionable. Honestly, given how infamous we are, I'm surprised they've overlooked it for as long as they have."

Koizumi's sensible position was accompanied by a smile that made me wonder which side he was on, anyway.

Put that way, I myself might've wanted to quibble with our arrangement, had I been on the council. But still—why now? The student council had thus far ignored the SOS Brigade like a lazy landlord neglecting to fix a leaky roof, I pointed out.

"They have indeed. However, the current council president may not be so easy to deal with."

Koizumi smiled, showing his white teeth, then looked at Nagato out of the corner of his eye.

Nagato, naturally, had no reaction, but she shifted her gaze from the end of the hallway down to my feet. It sort of seemed like she was apologizing for causing the trouble.

I, of course, did not feel like she was causing the trouble at all. Obviously. I knew only a single entity who inconvenienced the very air she moved through. The inconvenience's name was—

I exhaled and spoke the name.

"It's Haruhi's fault—like always."

It had been, ever since she'd announced that the space would henceforth be her clubroom.

"I'd ask you to keep this a secret from Suzumiya," said Koizumi. "I fear she would only complicate things. So after school, please make your way to the student council room without her seeing you."

Yeah, sure, I started to say, then stopped short at a strange detail.

"Wait just a minute. Why am *I* going? I'm not the kind of Johnny-come-lately who just wanders into a situation uninvited."

Of course, if Nagato asked me to go, I'd accompany her without a second thought, but Koizumi had no business asking me. Plus, if Nagato went alone, she'd be that much more likely to just scare the crap out of them, I figured.

"The council is well-informed. That's why I was appointed as messenger. I would be quite happy to act entirely as Nagato's representative, but should things go poorly, there could be problems later, and being her agent is not part of my job description. I suppose I can put it simply by saying: you are Suzumiya's representative."

"Why not just send Haruhi herself?"

"Are you being serious?" Koizumi exaggeratedly widened his eyes.

I answered his clumsy acting with a snort. If he wanted to know whether I understood the situation or not—yeah, I understood it. If we tossed a bomb like Haruhi in front of the student council, we'd be lucky if all we got was an explosion. Given the concern she'd shown for Nagato during the winter trip, if she found out Nagato had been called before the council, we'd only get as far as "Nagato's gotten a message from the student council…" before Haruhi would leap straight to breaking down the council room's door—or she might cut right to the chase and assault the staff room or the principal's office. Which might make her feel better, but I'd be the one to suffer afterward. Unlike Koizumi, I had no desire to transfer schools without any good reason.

"Well, then, I'll leave the matter in your hands." Koizumi smiled as though he'd known from the start what my answer would be. "I'll inform the student council president. We'll meet in the council room after school."

Koizumi's stride was light and long-legged as he walked away from classroom 5. When Haruhi wasn't around, he really did have quite an attitude. I watched Nagato follow behind him, feeling somehow that the end of our first year really was upon us.

At any rate, maybe Koizumi and Nagato were perfectly comfortable being the faces of the SOS Brigade. We were all cooperating, but the number of secrets we were keeping from Haruhi was increasing by the month…

Maybe I was being pointlessly sentimental.

Thanks to my sentimentality, I didn't get to ask Koizumi why he was going about normally as the student council's carrier pigeon.

Incidentally, the ever-perceptive Haruhi immediately picked up on my suspicious behavior—though she didn't realize it—during the break following fifth period.

A sharp object poked me in the back, and I turned around.

"What's got you so restless?" Haruhi demanded, twirling a mechanical pencil in her fingertips. "It's like someone's called you out or something."

I'd prepared a 100 percent unfalsifiable contingency plan for just such an occasion.

"Yeah, Okabe wanted me to see him. He went out of his way to call me over during the lunch break," I answered casually. "I guess there's some kind of problem with my grades. Depending on the final exam results, they might even be notifying my parents. He said that I have to change my ways now if I want to go on to college."

Of course, it didn't make sense to change my ways, given that nothing needed changing—not that I would've been able to anyway—but what I was saying wasn't complete nonsense. For one thing, Taniguchi'd gotten a similar earful, though not in so many words, and the conclusion I'd drawn after comparing notes with him was that our homeroom teacher was proportionally compassionate enough to be worried about his students' educational futures.

Of course, since I was pretty close to Taniguchi's level myself, we each had a sense that if one of us was slacking off, the other could afford to do so as well, which tended to dilute the feeling of tension. It was enough to make me think that Kunikida—who was careful to get decent grades—was the weird one.

"Huh?" Haruhi held her chin in her hands, elbows resting on her desk. "Were your grades that bad? I thought you were more serious about listening in class than I was," she said, gazing out the window. The speed of the passing clouds told of the wind's strength.

I would've appreciated not being lumped in with her brain. My own head didn't have anything to do with space-time distortions, data explosions, or monochrome parallel dimensions. Compared with Haruhi's unprecedented conceptions, it was a cute little miniature dachshund.

"Listening without comprehension is a waste of time," I said, without any particular conviction.

"Oh yeah?" Her eyes still fixed on the scenery outside the window, she spoke as though addressing the silent glass. "Should I help you out with studying, then? I don't mind—we'd just be going over the class material again. And I can definitely explain language arts better than they do in class.

"The teachers suck, after all," Haruhi murmured quietly to herself. She glanced at me, but then looked immediately away.

As I was trying to figure out how to answer—

"I mean, Mikuru's been freaking out too, right? This school's just a prefectural public school, but this time of year they get all weird and start acting like a prep school. It's really hard on the juniors. They've got all those special classes and mock exams and everything, and it turns their big class trip into a total mess. If that's what they're gonna do, they should move the class trip to freshman year. And the school festival should be in the spring, not fall, am I right?"

Despite her rapid-fire delivery, her eyes remained fixed on the drifting clouds. As she seemed to be waiting for a reply, I gave her one.

"Yeah, I guess," I agreed, looking at the clouds myself. "I just want to make it through the school year." Then, on the chance I got held back a year, I played up to Haruhi's ego and added, "Heya, Suzumiya-*senpai*."

"Kyon, you dork. Just go buy me some rolls. I'll pay you later."

I resented the prospect of such mundane conversations making their way into the clubroom. There wasn't anything wrong with getting Haruhi to make a test preparation guide in order to avoid that, right? Wait—it'd be good to have Nagato on the production staff too. I bet we could sell them for five hundred yen a pop, make a little money on the side. I figured I could cut Taniguchi a break and give him a bad-influence discount of 30 percent or so.

"No way," said Haruhi, immediately nixing the profitable-

sounding idea. "That wouldn't really help your academic ability at all. It would just be a temporary fix. If a slightly different question showed up on a test, you'd have no idea what to do. If you don't build up your knowledge properly, you'll fall for all their sneaky tricks. But don't worry. If you'll just apply yourself, I can get you to Kunikida's level in six months, easy."

I didn't really want her to get too enthusiastic about it. Despite my efforts not to, I found myself imagining the scene—sweating nervously as Haruhi *thwack*ed me on the head with a yellow megaphone, happily yelling at me, "No! Why can't you understand something so simple? What are you, an idiot?"

"I'll just ask you about the places I don't know," I said, "and all you have to do is explain those. I'll handle the rest myself somehow."

"If you can handle it yourself, why haven't you done that already?"

She certainly knew how to figure out the most annoying thing to say. She was dead right, I told her.

"Why're you being so stubborn?" Haruhi faced me, her lips tight with frustration, then leaned suddenly forward. "I won't allow the kind of scandal that would come from a member of the SOS Brigade failing out of school. That'd give the student council all the ammunition they'd need to come down on us. I need you to be just a tiny bit motivated so they don't get that opening. Got it?"

Haruhi's words were delivered with her brow furrowed in irritation, her mouth curving into a keen smile, glaring at me until my face showed acceptance of her demands.

Classes were over for the day.

I took my leave from Haruhi by pretending that I was headed for the staff room, then proceeded to the student council room. It was right next door to the staff room, so there was no need to take a detour, and soon I'd arrived at my destination.

Truth be told, now that I was here, I was feeling pretty nervous.

I didn't remember the student council president's face at all, even though I would've seen it during the council elections that came right after the school festival. I remembered hearing the candidates' speeches in the auditorium, but as a completely unaffiliated voter, I just picked the most mundane-sounding name on the ballot and immediately forgot it. What kind of person had it been? Whoever it was had to be at least a junior, since to be called "president" I figured you'd have to be an upperclassman of some kind. And surely it had to be someone with more dignity than the computer club president.

As I stood there hesitating in front of the door—

"Heya, Kyon! Whatcha doin'?"

A familiar long-haired figure popped out of the staff room. It was Asahina's classmate and an honorary adviser to the SOS Brigade, a junior girl who I knew by now was no ordinary individual.

No matter who you were, you had to tip your hat to her.

"'Sup," I said.

"Ha ha ha—'sup!" she replied to my jock-ish greeting.

Tsuruya raised both hands and smiled brilliantly, then looked at the door in front of which I stood.

"What's this? Got business with the student council?"

I was here to find out exactly what that business was, I explained. I'd never have business with them myself.

"Whaa?"

Tsuruya strode toward me vigorously—it was hard to say whether she or Haruhi was better at that—and despite my flinching away, put her mouth in close proximity to my ear.

"Hmm? Are you by some chance a student council spy?" she asked, in a quiet (by Tsuruya standards) voice.

I detected a hint of seriousness in Tsuruya's close-range smile. It was an expression I wasn't used to, given her standard of constant optimistic mirth. For some reason I felt compelled to explain myself.

"Um, well..."

*What do you want me to say, Tsuruya?* I pointed out that if I were a spy under orders from someone, I wouldn't be going to all this trouble at the moment.

"I guess that's true." Tsuruya stuck out her tongue. "Sorry for doubting ya! I just kinda overheard something, y'know? Know anything about the rumor that the student council's been over-run with people making secret deals behind the scenes? I hear it even goes back to the last election for council president. Not sure I buy it, though."

That was the first I'd heard of it. It was hard to imagine that kind of intrigue happening at our shabby little public school, so it was probably nothing more than a rumor. Although it did seem like the kind of academic drama that Haruhi would've loved.

"Tsuruya—what kind of person is the student council president?" I went ahead and asked her. It seemed like she might know more about the subject than I did.

I hoped she'd tell me something about his personality or something, but—

"I don't really know him very well. He's in a different class and all. He's sorta stuck up but also handsome, and pretty smart, from what I hear. If he were a character in the *Romance of the Three Kingdoms*, he'd be Sima Yi, that cunning army general. He's constantly working for more student independence, I hear, since the last student council was out of touch—total pie-in-the-sky."

It was troubling that despite the reference to a famous historical figure, I couldn't easily imagine his personality—and the comparison to airborne pie was suspicious, as well.

"Uh, by the way—why were you in the staff room?"

"Hmm? Oh, it's my turn to deliver the weekly reports, so I came by to do that," she said easily, slapping my back and purposefully raising her voice. "Anyway, Kyon, good luck! If you're gonna wrestle with the student council, I've got your back! I'm an ally to all in Haru-nyan's club!"

It was certainly reassuring. However, I didn't want things to go that far. There was no telling what methods the ecstatic Haruhi would employ upon the appearance of a truly worthy adversary. It exhausted my mental capacity just thinking about it. And as things stood, I already had enough to worry about.

Tsuruya waved her hand in a good-bye gesture, and having said everything she wanted to say, strode off briskly.

As usual, she'd gotten to the heart of the matter without my saying anything. In that sense, her cognitive abilities rivaled even Haruhi's. She was probably the only person at North High who could demonstrate power equivalent to Haruhi's in a matchup. The difference between her and our pain-in-the-neck brigade chief was that Tsuruya hadn't left her common sense behind.

Given the thin construction of the wall and door, though, it was a safe bet that her last words had been audible on the inside. There *was* something Haruhi-like hidden within her, in the end.

Oh, well—it was time to gird my loins and do this.

I gave the door a polite knock to avoid offending whoever was inside.

"Enter," came a sudden voice from within the room.

It was surprising to hear somebody actually commanding me to "enter," especially in a voice so deep and severe you'd expect to hear it overdubbing some famous veteran actor in a foreign movie.

I slid the door open and entered the student council room for the first time in my life.

While it boasted a slightly larger size than the literature club's room, it wasn't that much different than any other room in the

old building. In fact, without a triangular plaque reading Council President on one of the desks, it felt a little drab compared
with our room. It was really nothing more than a meeting room.

Koizumi, having arrived before I did, greeted me. "I'm glad you
made it."

Standing next to Koizumi, evidently also having waited for me,
was Nagato.

"..."

Nagato cast her clever gaze toward the window, in front of
which stood the president.

He was... how to put it?

It was obvious enough that he was a tall male student. For
whatever reason, he was looking out the window, his hands
clasped behind him, not so much as moving a muscle. His form
was indistinct, backlit as it was by the afternoon sun that
streamed through the south-facing window.

There was another person, sitting at one corner of the room's
long table. It was a female student, face downturned over an
opened notebook, mechanical pencil in hand, poised for record-
ing the proceedings. Apparently she was the secretary.

The president did not move. I had no idea what was so fascinating about the scenery visible from the window—all you could
see from there were the tennis courts and the totally abandoned
swimming pool—but the meaningful silence dragged on.

"Mr. President," Koizumi finally said after an appropriate
interval, his voice brimming with fresh solicitousness. "All the
individuals you asked to come have arrived. Feel free to proceed
with your business."

The president slowly turned, at which point I finally beheld his
face. He was a second-year student, and he wore a slim-framed pair
of glasses. He was a pretty handsome guy, but not like Koizumi's
dime-store-teen-idol good looks. There was a callous look in his
eye, like a young and upwardly mobile professional whose every

thought was turned toward improving his own position. I reflexively anticipated that I would not get along with him very well.

His face expressionless—but not like Nagato's—he spoke. "I believe you have already heard this, Koizumi, but I'll state it again. The reason all of you are here is quite simple. The student council is giving the literature club its final notice."

Final notice? Had we ever been given a notice at all? If we had, I couldn't imagine Nagato had meekly complied with their summons, which was what had allowed us to continue using the clubroom as our base of operations.

" . . . "

Unconcerned with Nagato's lack of response, the president coldly continued.

"Currently you are the literature club in name only. Is this correct?"

I guess holing up in the clubroom and reading books wasn't good enough.

" . . . "

Nagato said nothing.

"You are no longer a functioning student organization."

" . . . "

Nagato silently regarded the president.

"I'll be clear. The findings of our inquiry are this: we of the student council do not currently see any purpose in the existence of the literature club."

" . . . "

Nagato was very still.

"Thus, I am informing you of the immediate and indefinite suspension of the literature club. You will promptly vacate your clubroom."

" . . . "

Nagato remained silent, as though she didn't care one way or another. But I knew better.

"Miss…Nagato, was it?" The president calmly returned Nagato's tangible gaze. "There are non–club members in your room, and you've allowed them to stay there. And I wonder what you've done with the budget provided to the literature club this year. Would you suggest that your film counts as a literary activity? According to my investigation, that film was produced by and credited to the SOS Brigade, an unauthorized organization, and the literature club's name appears nowhere on it. And the film itself was made without the permission of the school festival's organization committee."

It was painful to hear. Perhaps because Koizumi and Nagato never had any intention of stopping Haruhi, the responsibility of restraining her tyranny fell solely to me. And there was Asahina to think about as well—forced to play the powerless heroine.

"…"

Nagato's profile did not suggest any assertiveness on her part, though that was just an amateur's observation.

Perhaps taking her silence as a sign of acquiescence, the president maintained his pompous demeanor.

"The literature club's activities will be temporarily suspended, and you will remain prohibited from entering the clubroom until such time as new members can be recruited next year. Are there any complaints? Feel free to voice them. We will listen, if nothing else."

"…"

Nagato didn't move a muscle, but Haruhi, Asahina, or Koizumi would've understood what was going on. And if that crowd could understand, then it would be obvious to me. That much I could gather.

"…"

Nagato, sunken into silence.

"…"

Nagato, quietly furious.

"Hmph. You have no objections, then?" The president curled the corner of his lips unpleasantly. "The literature club has but one member—you, Miss Nagato. You are effectively the club president. If you'll consent, in order to preserve the clubroom, we can immediately begin the removal of all foreign objects from it. Such objects will either be disposed of or stored by us. Any personal items must be immediately removed—"

"Now wait just a second." I interrupted the president's monologue before Nagato's silent rage reached critical levels. "You can't just suddenly say stuff like that. It's not fair to ignore us for so long, then drop this on us out of nowhere."

"Oh, is that so?" The president regarded me with a cold glare, snickering. "I've had a look at the Student Organization Establishment Form you submitted. It's like a bad joke. If we approved every organization whose goals were so absurd, there would be no end to it."

The sneering, haughty upperclassman pushed his glasses up in an exaggeratedly dramatic fashion.

"You should learn better rhetoric. In fact, you should probably devote yourself more to academics in general. I can't imagine your grades are so good that you can afford to be wasting so much time after school playing around with this ridiculous 'club.'"

So that *was* it. The president's real goal all along had been to destroy the SOS Brigade. All this nonsense about the literature club was just a pretense. At least Ultra Director Haruhi had managed to come up with some kind of an excuse to put Nagato in her movie's script—this guy wasn't even bothering.

"And don't tell me you'll just join the literature club," said the president, heading off an option that hadn't even occurred to me yet. "Consider this: even if you all had been good-faith members of the literature club, you have not done a single thing that can be remotely recognized as literary activity. Just what *have* you been doing, I wonder?"

The president's glasses glittered pointlessly. What was that, some kind of special effect?

"And yet we have been tolerant. The 'SOS Brigade,' as you call it, was established without permission and has simply acted as it pleased. Detonating fireworks on the school roof, threatening faculty, wandering around the campus in lascivious clothing, cooking stew in a building with a no-open-flames policy—these would be unacceptable for *any* club. Just who do you think you are, exactly?"

I could see that everything he was saying was totally accurate. That was all on us. We should've at least asked about these things first. I seriously doubted we would've been given permission, but we sure weren't going to just roll over and do what they wanted now.

"This is dirty pool," I said, inheriting Nagato's fury. "If that's your problem, you should've just gone straight to Haruhi. What's the point of bringing in Nagato and threatening to dissolve the lit club?"

The president had anticipated this tack. "It should be obvious, shouldn't it?" He was totally unperturbed, folding his arms and speaking as though he was an elite executive who'd just finished reading a proposal written by an inept subordinate. "The SOS Brigade does not exist as a student organization. Am I mistaken?"

Had it really come to this?

No matter how hard the student council or its president tried, they could not dissolve the SOS Brigade—because administratively speaking, no such brigade existed in the school. Trying to make something that didn't exist disappear was like multiplying by zero; the answer was still always zero. Even if it didn't go badly and wind up being analogous to multiplying a negative by a negative, you never knew what was going to happen if you poked Haruhi Suzumiya wrong. She might go flying off in any direction. Her behavior was totally unpredictable, like a hooked ball heading for a 7-10 split that jumps into a different lane for a 10-pin strike.

If you tried to throw the straight-on fastball at a girl like that, she'd just smash a line drive foul into your dugout—basically, it was pointless, or so the student council must have concluded when they'd decided to lay their indirect siege.

Which they did by attacking the third-floor clubroom of the literature club, which the SOS Brigade was illegally occupying.

If the literature club could be summoned and brought to task, then the SOS Brigade's residence would automatically disappear. The only reason we were allowed to use the clubroom was because the sole real literature club member had said, "It's fine," and Nagato was probably the only person who would've said so when asked if her clubroom could be borrowed.

If the literature club was dissolved, Nagato would cease to be a member, and her days of quietly reading in the room would be over, and the five of us would no longer have anywhere to go after school.

It was a magnificent tactic. I was impressed. The worst part was no matter what we did, Nagato became both victim and coconspirator.

I knew how weak our position was, which gave me no way to formulate a counterargument. Haruhi would've done it anyway, and all I could do was wonder if the president knew that, but in any case it made summoning Nagato the obvious course of action.

Nagato, meanwhile, seemed to be reaching her limit.

" . . . "

The silent pressure emanating from the petite, school-uniformed figure was tangibly filling the room. I wondered what would happen if we just let her go. I doubted the world would be rewritten, but I could imagine the student council president with his memory erased, being controlled like a puppet. Or perhaps she'd do what she did after the Asakura debacle, using data manipulation to transform both the president and the clubroom into something completely different. When Yuki Nagato went on a rampage, there was no telling what could happen. I was inescapably reminded of last fall's contest against the computer club.

The president took a step back and posed in front of the setting sun. Just as I was nervously thinking about telling him just how much trouble he'd gotten himself into—

"..."

Silent as ever, the invisible feeling of menace disappeared.

"Hmm?"

The aura I (thought I had) detected from Nagato had vanished, as though it had never been there. I couldn't help but glance at Nagato, whose unblinking gaze had shifted from the president to a different individual.

I followed her eyes.

The presumably second-year girl whose pencil had been moving as she'd taken notes during the meeting slowly looked up from her writing.

"...Huh?" I said stupidly.

I immediately wondered why *she* was here, then realized I couldn't remember her name. It had been last summer. A strange incident that happened a bit after Tanabata. I'd never forget what I'd seen, but in the end it hadn't really mattered...

"Is something the matter?" the president asked haughtily. "Ah, I haven't introduced you. This is the student council's top officer, and she's taking notes for me today—"

The girl's hair shifted slightly as she bowed.

"—Miss Emiri Kimidori."

The massive cave cricket came thundering back into my mind.

"Kimidori?"

This girl who'd gotten involved in a truly ridiculous chain of events that had started with the SOS Brigade website, then moved

on into investigating the disappearance of the computer club president, and finally ended up in a different dimension, was now seated in a corner of the student council room, looking at us as though she didn't recognize us at all.

Kimidori smiled pleasantly, shifting her gaze from me to Nagato. I got the feeling that her eyes narrowed just a bit—and that she and Nagato had exchanged some kind of sign. I even thought I noticed Nagato give a tiny, reluctant nod.

What was this? Had some kind of telepathic signal passed between the two of them?

The more I thought about it, the stranger that incident seemed. Kimidori had claimed to be the computer club president's girl-friend, but then the president himself had told us he didn't even have a girlfriend. So as to the question of what reasoning had led Kimidori to turn to the SOS Brigade for counseling, I'd just assumed it had been Nagato's doing. But now bumping into her again and seeing her exchange looks with Nagato—I couldn't imagine it was a coincidence.

I was as terrified as a young Slavic soldier hearing the sounds of a squadron of Luftwaffe dive-bombers.

*Wham—!*

From behind me echoed a sudden noise, like a balloon burst-ing. My heart attempted to leap free of the confines of my rib cage and leave me behind—

"Hey!"

There was no mistaking the hundred-decibel voice that sounded its war cry through the now-open door of the student council room. The voice continued at its eardrum-rattling volume.

"What does this pathetic excuse for a student council think it's doing, locking up my three faithful servants in a room like this? I figured you'd get around to doing something sooner or later, but if it was going to be this interesting, you should've just come straight to me! And what's this? Don't tell me you're giving Yuki

26

a hard time. Kyon would be one thing, but there's no way you're getting away with hurting Yuki! I'll beat the stuffing out of you and toss you right out the window!"

Yes, indeed, there was but one individual who could come breaking in there like a mother cat whose kittens have been threatened.

I didn't have to turn around to know who it was, but I wanted to see the look on her face. Yup, it was her, looking even livelier than usual, elation practically radiating off her at having found something so interesting.

"You can't keep me out of this, you know. I'm the supreme leader of the SOS Brigade!" Haruhi boasted. A moment later, her eyes alighted upon the level's final boss. Her pupils, shining with the force of whole galactic clusters, took in the shape of the lanky, bespectacled boy. "So you're the student council president? Very well, I accept your challenge. It's president vs. brigade chief, so the fight money's even. No objections, right?"

Then she turned to me, as though to take me to task for harboring such pointless questions as how she'd even found out we were here. "And you, Kyon! Don't tell me you're just going to shut up and let this happen. Don't hold back just because it's the student council president. If we all jump him at once, then tie him up, the rest will be cake. I'll put him in a joint lock, so just get some rope ready!"

Her eyes blazed, brimming with lava that threatened to form a caldera right on the spot.

"..."

In contrast to that, like a front-line commander, Nagato was silently ignoring the sudden and unasked-for reinforcements, still not moving as she observed Kimidori with her dormant-volcano eyes.

Instead of jumping the student council president or scampering off in search of some rope, I simply watched the expression of the person who was facing the brunt of this intruder's threat.

It was strange. The president's brow creased as he directed an accusatory glance at the person standing next to me—Koizumi. For some reason I thought I noticed him shake his head slightly. With a pained smile on Koizumi's face, it seemed the two of them had shared some kind of silent communication, and I suddenly wished I'd never noticed anything at all.

"What are you trying to pull, anyway? If you're going to call out somebody, call me! Trying to cut the brigade chief out of all this, are you? Some student council you are!"

"Suzumiya, please calm down." Koizumi casually put his hand on Haruhi's shoulder. "Let us at least hear the council out. We're still in the middle of the conversation."

He—suspiciously—made eye contact with me. Was I supposed to know what the hell to do?

The only thing I knew was that our brigade chief had come to her underlings' rescue in their time of need.

"Fine, then it's come to all-out war! I'll warn you that we're happy to take on any challenge, any time, any place. Every single member of the SOS Brigade is a valiant warrior, who knows neither fear nor mercy, and you shall receive none till you either weep or kneel!"

I got the feeling that the situation was only going to escalate.

And it was already bad enough, with Tsuruya offering her support in advance, Nagato right on the verge of exploding, and the unexpected and sudden return of Kimidori.

Plus, Koizumi and the student council president were part of the picture too, somehow.

"Kyon, what're you doing? We're up against the student council president! It's the most obvious enemy we've ever had! If we're not going to do battle here, where would we fight? At least give him a harsher look!"

Student council vs. SOS Brigade, huh?

Someone, somewhere, had triggered the switch for this event—a switch I wished they'd ignored. I really hoped it hadn't been me.

I wondered what was going to happen next as I regarded Haruhi, who was infuriated but also somehow delighted. Whatever it was, the certainty that it wouldn't be good news swirled within my chest.

"Oh brother," I muttered under my breath. I'd like to think it was an understandable reaction.

And in fact, the situation turned into the exact opposite of good news.

Haruhi underwent a class switch from "brigade chief" to "editor in chief," ordering us Brigade members to become authors and write pseudonovels, a task so random and unprecedented it was like a Stinger anti-aircraft missile trying to target a Jupiter Ghost Gundam.

Haruhi was like a short-fused street fighter who'd picked up a letter of challenge meant for somebody else and had come to the fighting arena anyway. "Come on, mister evil student council president! Are you up for a no-holds-barred, no-referee, no-rules, winner-takes-all fight?" she shouted in a high-handed voice, her finger pointed accusatorially at the president, whose back was to the window.

The president didn't even try to hide his irritated expression. "Miss Suzumiya. I don't know what sort of techniques you're accustomed to using in your fights, but I'm not in the habit of walking into a ring my enemy's prepared for me. The 'rules' you've proposed are the epitome of barbarism. It is unbecoming. Know this: the student council cannot allow fights on the school grounds, no matter the reason."

Haruhi's gaze never left the president's face. "So what challenge would you have us face? Mah-jongg? You can even bring a pinch hitter to stand in for you; I don't care. Or maybe you'd prefer a computer game? I've got just the game."

"There will be no mah-jongg and no video games." The president deliberately removed his glasses, polishing them with a handkerchief before putting them back on. "There will be no challenges at all. I have no time to play along with your games."

Haruhi began to boldly stride forth, but I held her back with a hand on her shoulder. "Hold on, Haruhi. Who told you we were in here?" I asked.

Haruhi glared at me belligerently. "I heard from Mikuru. She said she'd heard it from Tsuruya. As soon as I'd heard that the student council president had called you guys in, I came right over—Yuki and Koizumi were missing from the clubroom too, after all. I knew right away that the student council was finally making its move. They knew they'd lose if they went up against me, so they attacked our weak spot. Just the kind of cheap move I'd expect from a petty villain."

The president didn't move, even when called a "petty villain." The second-year student seemed more bored than anything else as he looked at Haruhi, then finally voiced another complaint to Koizumi.

"Mr. Koizumi. Perhaps you should explain—explain why it was that I summoned Miss Nagato."

"Yes, Mr. President," said Koizumi calmly, his smile chagrined. He did so love explaining things.

"I don't need any explanations," said Haruhi, cutting him right off. "You're just trumping up charges to destroy the literature club, since if Yuki's not a club member anymore, then we won't be able to use the room. You probably figured since she's such a nice, quiet girl you'd be able to just talk circles around her, but I won't have it. If you've got a problem with the SOS Brigade, don't bother with this sneaky crap—just say it to our faces!"

As she went on, Haruhi's own words incited her to greater

enthusiasm. She went into kicking stance, as though she was preparing for a throw down. And you had to hand it to her—her intuition was excellent. Just as I was thinking that Koizumi would be disappointed at not getting to explain anything—

"Thank you for saving me the time of explaining. That is indeed the situation," said Koizumi, his facade of serenity unperturbed. "However, we are still in the midst of negotiations. I expect the president has not finished speaking. In any case, forcing an officially sanctioned club like the literature club to suspend its activities immediately, with no grace period, cannot be possible. I don't believe the student council has the authority to do that. Does it, Mr. President?"

So he *had* gotten to make his explanation. Just as I was thinking this third-rate melodrama couldn't get any worse, the president put on his best honor-student-in-a-cheap-melodrama face.

"Naturally, we of the student council do not wish to cause unnecessary conflict. If the literature club were to conduct standard literary activities, we would have no complaints at all. What we find problematic is the fact that there have been no such activities."

"Does that mean we have an alternative to immediate suspension?" asked Koizumi immediately.

"It is not an alternative; it is a requirement," said the president huffily. "You must immediately engage in at least one activity befitting the literature club. If you do, we'll lift the indefinite suspension and approve continued use of the clubroom."

Haruhi lowered her raised foot, though her voice and demeanor remained confrontational. "So you can see reason, then. Will you approve the SOS Brigade as well? And not just as an informal association—as a true student organization. If you did that, we'd be entitled to our share of an operating budget."

I recalled that being written in the student handbook. But the student council president was not so foolish as to let a random

"Brigade" that wasn't even an informal association jump two levels overnight. "I know of no such brigade. And I can't possibly allow said brigade to be recognized as a club, nor portion it any of the school's meager budget."

The president folded his arms slowly, unconcerned as he returned Haruhi's angry glare. There wasn't so much as a single drop of sweat on him, so he clearly wasn't bluffing. Where had he found such confidence?

"I'd prefer to hear as little talk about 'brigades' as possible. We are discussing the literature club. Whatever unauthorized group you choose to form on your own is none of my concern. The only reason it reached my ears in the first place was because of the disruption in the literature club's operation. I'd like never to be troubled by it again."

He should've just left us alone then, given that no matter how sneaky and circumspect his methods, it would be only a matter of time before Haruhi came barging into the student council room. She'd do it before the day was out, and she'd be dragging me along by my necktie behind her.

"As for the literature club, obviously not just any activity will do. Using the room for a reading group or for writing book reports on library books—such things belong in elementary school. I will not approve them."

"So what're you telling us to do?" Haruhi cocked her head slightly, her eyes still blazing. "Kyon, what does a literature club even do besides reading? Do you know?"

"Beats me" was my honest answer. She'd be better off asking Nagato.

"There is but one requirement," said the president, ignoring our conversation. "Creating a publication. Past generations of the literature club have all managed to create at least one publication a year, even during times of low membership. We have the records. It is the most visible activity you can do. The literature club is, quite literally, about the art of literature. Simple reading is not enough."

Which meant that all this time, Nagato hadn't been acting like a proper club member. Our little Nagato had only ever read books.

I couldn't help but shake my head. I didn't want to think about her troubled, bespectacled face as she sat in front of an obsolete PC. Seeing it in my dreams was enough.

"Any objections?"

The president seemed to have misread my expression. In any case, he looked like he had objections aplenty.

"Bear in mind that this is the most minimal possible concession. By all rights, we should've given you notice at the school festival. I'd like you to feel a bit of gratitude at my having waited this long. Of course, anybody else would've left you alone indefinitely."

Nagato aside, I wished he would've left Haruhi out of it, I told him.

"That would not have done. I won election to the student council on my promises for school reform. As you know, the previous council was a council in name only, and there was little allowance made for student independence. It simply followed the plans handed down by the school administration. It was an insubstantial organization that did only as it was told." The president casually tossed off this heated rhetoric. "I aimed to free the council from that position. If the students wished it, the cafeteria menu should be expanded and enriched, the most trivial matters remaining up for discussion—I planned to negotiate with the school to make that a reality."

I was grateful for this work on the student body's behalf, but if that were true, why wouldn't he hear a single student's desire to have "brigade" added to the official organization list, along with "association" and "club," I asked him.

"My slogan is 'Serious reform.' If I were to publicly acknowledge such a frivolous organization, it would destroy my reputation. I cannot allow it," said the president, refusing my request. "Your deadline is in one week. One week from today you must present two hundred copies of a literature club newsletter. If you do not, the club will be suspended and the room vacated. I will hear no objections on this matter."

A newsletter? I wondered if that was anything like an anthology.

"Fine," Haruhi agreed. It wasn't her line, though—Nagato should've been the one to say so.

Nagato, of course, was silent, and she seemed unlikely to say anything, so I supposed it was all right for Haruhi to speak in her place, but something about the particular nature of Nagato's silence at the moment made me think it was different from her usual taciturnity.

"..."

All the while, Nagato faced Kimidori, neither of them looking away from the other. Nagato was expressionless, while Kimidori had a thin smile.

I wasn't sure why, but maybe it was fortunate that Haruhi didn't seem to notice Kimidori, the SOS Brigade's very first client. Apparently Haruhi was too busy glaring at the president to pay any attention to the secretary. Or maybe she just didn't remember the face. She hadn't seen that cave cricket, after all.

"A newsletter, eh?" said Haruhi with an expression like a mathematician who had just proven a theorem. "Is that like a zine? With stories, essays, columns, poems—stuff like that, right?"

"The contents are none of my concern," said the president. "You are free to use the printing room and may write whatever you wish. However, there is another condition. The completed newsletter will be set out on a table in the main hallway, and that is all. You may not hand it out or solicit readers. Bunny girls are out. If you cannot give away all two hundred from that table within three days, there will be a penalty."

"What kind of penalty?" asked Haruhi, her eyes shining. She did so love her punishment games.

"We will let you know when the time comes," said the president, annoyed. "But be prepared. There are a number of ways to use volunteer work. I will say it again—this is a concession."

The president seemed to be worried about unilaterally bringing about the tragic end of a clan. You didn't have to know the history of the Ako domain to guess that much—especially not when your opponent was Haruhi. And I doubted Haruhi would be satisfied with just the head of the president. If things went badly, the school itself would be scattered to the wind.

I will leave it for future generations to decide whether the student council truly gave in or not, but in any case this "club newsletter" business was certainly their way of evading the issue.

And while Koizumi might have worked for the Agency, he was no literary agent, which meant the literature club would have to step up. And as an activity of the literature club, the newsletter had to have literary merit of some kind, but what did that even mean? Who was going to write it, and what would he or she write? And why was Haruhi looking so bizarrely delighted?

"Well, isn't this interesting!" She grinned like a child who'd discovered a new game. "Call it a bulletin, a newsletter, or a zine—if you say we've gotta make it, then we're gonna make it. This is for Yuki, after all. Can't have the Lit Club disappearing. That clubroom is mine, and I hate it when people take my stuff."

Haruhi's hand reached for the nape of Nagato's neck—not mine, for once.

"Well, since it's decided, we've gotta have a meeting. Yuki, we'll put your name in the masthead as publisher. I'll do everything else, of course, so don't worry about that. First we've got to go learn how to make a newsletter!"

Haruhi grabbed the back of Nagato's collar.

"..."

Nagato was pulled wordlessly along, and easily too, as though she were a balloon. Haruhi opened the door with a *clunk*, then dashed out through it like a bullet from a rifle.

I looked over my shoulder and saw Nagato's feet disappear through the doorway, and then she was gone, dragged out by Haruhi, who'd barged into the room like a strong wind but left like a typhoon gaining strength.

"Such an obnoxious girl," observed the president accurately, shaking his head, then looking down at the table beside him. "Miss Kimidori, we're finished here. You may leave."

"Yes, Mr. President." Kimidori nodded politely, closing her notebook and standing. She put the notebook back on its shelf, nodding briefly at the president before walking out of the room.

She gave me a brief bow as she passed by, walking through the door that Haruhi had opened without meeting my eyes. Her hair fluttered a bit as she went, a pleasant scent wafting behind her. I found myself a bit dizzy.

As I was pondering the nature of Nagato and Kimidori's relationship, the president snorted and spoke.

"Koizumi, close the door."

His tone was very different from a moment ago, and I turned my gaze back toward him.

The president watched Koizumi close and lock the door, then roughly sat down on a nearby folding chair and put his feet up on the desk.

*What the hell?*

But it was too early for me to be surprised, because the president then furrowed his brow as he rummaged in his uniform's pocket for something. By the time I realized that he'd produced a lighter and cigarette, he already had the cigarette between his lips, a curl of smoke beginning to rise from it.

It certainly didn't seem like the kind of thing the student council president should be doing. Just as I was beginning to feel like I'd discovered a firefighter committing arson—

"That'll about do it, right, Koizumi?" said the president, cigarette in mouth as he removed his glasses, put them in his pocket, and took out a portable ashtray. "The plan changed a little, but I pretty much did what you wanted—but damn, keeping up that stupid act was a pain in the ass. You gotta put yourself in my place. Talking in that serious freakin' voice all the time really takes it outta me."

The president's cool demeanor had completely changed as he exhaled smoke and tapped the cigarette's ash into the ashtray.

"Student council president, my ass. I never wanted the job! Pain in the neck, if you ask me. And then I gotta deal with that flighty broad. Ridiculous damn work."

In only a moment, the president had turned sulky and peevish. He put the stinky, smoking cigarette out on the edge of the ashtray, then got out another one and turned his attention to me. "You want one?"

"I'll pass." I shook my head, then looked over at the serenely smiling Koizumi standing next to me. "So the president's one of your guys?"

I'd sort of figured as much. They'd exchanged suspicious eye contact, plus if you'd really wanted to contact the literature club, you'd skip Koizumi and just go straight for Nagato. I didn't even have to think about it hard—there was no reason for the student council to go to the trouble of calling me in either.

Koizumi returned my look, making a show of smiling as he answered.

"I suppose you could say that, but he is not an associate in the same way that Mr. Arakawa or Miss Mori are. He is not directly connected with the Agency." Koizumi glanced at the president, the smoke from his second cigarette now rising to the ceiling.

"He is our confederate within the school, cooperating with us in exchange for certain considerations. If Mori, Arakawa, and I are the inner circle, you could consider him the outer circle."

I didn't care who was in what circle—how did a guy like this get to be student council president, I wanted to know.

"You could say it was the result of an extreme effort on my part, considering his lack of motivation. I had to make him a candidate, position him to gain the favor of the constituency over the previous council's recommended nominee, and constantly maneuver to win the majority in the election for president. It took quite a bit of work, all told."

I was bored already.

"The amount of money it required to win the presidency was probably about as much as it would take a minor political party to run for office in the lower Diet house."

Now it had gone beyond boring and was actively sapping my will to live.

"Going by what Koizumi here said," said the president, ill-temperedly exhaling smoke, "I had to become president before that stupid girl Suzumiya—or whatever her name is—got the idea in her head to try it herself. I wound up getting tapped thanks to my 'presidential face.' Friggin' ridiculous. I even had to wear these fake glasses."

The conversation had long since turned tiresome.

"Upon fully considering what Suzumiya's image of a student council president would be, the closest match of that image in this school was him. In this case, his disposition was irrelevant. The only thing that mattered was his looks."

And he'd made the mistake of falling for Koizumi's spiel.

He was tall, handsome, and bespectacled—a pointlessly haughty upperclassman. His role was to play a Haruhi-esque villain who would abuse student council power to deal with a small-time humanities club.

He was every inch the quick and easy villain that Haruhi would've wanted him to be.

But the fact that Koizumi had needed to go to such lengths in order to create the antagonist that was Haruhi's fondest wish meant that she wasn't truly omnipotent. If she was indeed all-knowing and all-powerful, it would've been the simplest thing in the world, wouldn't it? I asked Koizumi whether all his effort didn't mean exactly that.

"Ah, but the result of our labor was the creation of exactly the student council president that Haruhi wanted, which means that her wish did in fact become reality, does it not? Practically speaking, it does."

He was talking circles around me again. Only Tsuruya was better at it than he was.

The president irritably crushed out his cigarette. "Anyway, Koizumi. Next year *you* be the president. If what you want is to avoid Suzumiya running for the job, then just do it yourself."

"I wonder about that. I'm fairly busy myself, and lately I feel as though Suzumiya wouldn't make a bad president herself."

The hell she wouldn't. If Haruhi set out to conquer the school, there was no telling what would happen. I had a feeling that it would wind up being a huge pain for the rest of the brigade too. She might decide to give the entire student body the SOS Brigade treatment. Knowing her, she'd probably decide that, since she was president, the rest of the students were now her subordinates. The whole school would turn into an alternate dimension.

Still, so long as the election was carried out correctly, I couldn't imagine that Haruhi would actually win. I still believed in the average North High student's sense of common decency. So long as Koizumi didn't pull some kind of stunt, no election could possibly result in Haruhi winning high office.

I sighed. "So basically, Koizumi, this is another one of your games, is what you're telling me. You've just invented this 'student council plotting to destroy the literature club' scenario to give Haruhi something to do."

"It was no more than the seed, though." Koizumi exhaled a sigh into the drifting smoke. "There are a number of outcomes that are now possible. All will be well if we finish our publication by the deadline, but if we cannot finish, or if we fail to meet the requirements…" He shrugged lightly. "If that time comes, we'll just think of a different game to play. I'll be counting on your brain for that too."

I was happy enough to participate as an observer, but I sure wasn't interested in trying to think of new challenges that I myself would have to face. What could I possibly have to gain from that? I wanted to know.

"As far as my being the student council president goes," said the punk prez, "it definitely has its perks. First of all, it makes my school record look great. Of all the reasons Koizumi used to try to talk me into it, that was the biggest one. You said you'd get me through the college entrance exams, right? You better not have forgotten about that."

"Of course not. I remember. We're making the arrangements, naturally."

The president eyed Koizumi suspiciously, as though he were interrogating a suspect. He then sniffed. "You'd better be. Doing this ridiculous job has been a pain in the ass, but I've learned some things in the last few months. The student council really has been totally useless so far. It might as well not exist. Which means I can mess around with it as much as I want."

The president then smiled for the very first time. There was a certain degree of malice in it, but it was more a human expression than it was a calculating one.

"'Uphold student independence' really is a great slogan. Depending on the interpretation, it can mean anything. That budget is especially interesting, let me tell you. I'll bet there are some delicious details in there."

Some president we had. He was definitely up to Haruhi's expectations of villainy.

"We'll permit a modest abuse of authority," said Koizumi, miffed. "But please do not get carried away. There is a limit to how much support we can provide."

"Oh, I know. I won't pull anything that'd get the teachers' attention—I'd lose my hold on the sympathies of the council. I've already swept away the remaining members of the student council. There's no one left to oppose me."

I was starting to like this president guy. He was obviously up to no good, but for some reason he was strangely compelling. It was a little strange to be feeling as though following him would be all right, but...

Suddenly alarm bells went off as Tsuruya's face appeared in my mind. I remembered what she'd told me when I'd encountered her in the hallway. Her keen, almost extrasensory perception had told her that the student council and its president had a hidden agenda. The student council's spy—that wasn't me, Tsuruya; it was Koizumi. He was more than a spy, though; he was a puppet master.

I didn't particularly care if the president used his powers to his own advantage, but if Haruhi realized it, she might press for an immediate recall and recommend Tsuruya as his replacement. I could imagine Tsuruya laughing heartily and charging straight in, right along with her. Koizumi and I would automatically wind up being on Haruhi's side too, and the president would be overthrown.

I wish you luck in your future secret maneuverings, Mr. President. Just keep them where we can't see them.

He probably didn't need me to tell him that, though. And while his role would probably bring him into occasional conflict with Haruhi, I just wanted him to choose his battles carefully.

I walked out of the student council room side-by-side with Koizumi, then remembered there was something I needed to ask him.

"So I understand that the president is under your supervision. But what about the secretary? Is Kimidori one of your confederates too?"

"She is not," said Koizumi, like it was nothing. "Kimidori took the secretary post rather unexpectedly. The truth is that when I thought to check, she was already there, which is why I hadn't noticed until that point—even though I feel that in the early days of the current student council administration, we'd appointed a different student to that position. But when I checked later, all the records said she was there from the start. Even my memory. Nobody, not even the president, has any doubts about it. If it is a case of falsification, it's an extraordinary example of such."

If it were so extraordinary, I asked, why didn't he sound a little more surprised?

"If I were surprised to such an extent, if anything more unexpected were to happen, I might very well go into cardiac arrest." Koizumi turned his head to regard the windows as we walked leisurely down the hall. "Emiri Kimidori is one of Nagato's comrades. That much is unmistakable."

I'd figured as much. Her coming to us with the cave-cricket trouble had been too perfect of a coincidence. If it had been just that, I might've believed that Nagato had set up the whole thing herself, but given the current situation, our previous encounter could hardly have been an accident. What worried me was not knowing how closely Nagato and Kimidori were tied.

"There was the trouble with Ryoko Asakura, yes. But I don't think we need to worry too much on that count. It seems that

Kimidori and Nagato are comparatively closely related. At the very least, they do not oppose each other."

How did he know that? They didn't *look* like they got along very well. Although they didn't look like they got along especially poorly either, I admitted.

"We in the Agency would like to test our intelligence-gathering capabilities. We contacted some—not many but a few—TFEIs like Nagato, in an effort to convey our intentions. While they were by no means cooperative, we can make some deductions based on the fragmentary conversations. It seems that a different faction within the Data Overmind sent Kimidori than the one Nagato is associated with. But we know that, unlike Ryoko Asakura, they are not hostile."

I wasn't sure what to think of the things I heard Koizumi saying so casually, but it wasn't anything new, so neither of us was particularly worried.

Still, I'd known there were different kinds of aliens, but to think that Kimidori was one of them...Given the way she'd calmed down the furious Nagato in the student council room, perhaps her faction was a peaceful one, I said.

"Quite possibly. We have concluded that there is no need to be excessively conscious of her movements. In my opinion, Kimidori's role is to observe Nagato. I don't know how long it's been the case, but that seems to be the job she's currently settled into."

Koizumi's voice sounded like he was in the middle of climbing a mountain during a long hike, so I didn't press him on the matter. As far as Nagato went, I had quite a few memories of her myself, many of which I preferred not to share. Even if he was a member of the SOS Brigade, Koizumi wasn't someone I wanted to explain these things to over and over again. I'd play them back in my head as many times as I wanted to, though.

I fell vaguely into silence as we walked quickly to the clubroom, Koizumi likewise keeping his mouth shut.

When you get a rapid input of strange information, it seems like the last things you hear are the most memorable.

Which is why I hadn't forgotten.

I hadn't forgotten that Haruhi, having snatched Nagato and flown out of the student council room, was in there.

I was just kind of spaced out, thinking about everything— about the outlaw student council president and about Kimidori.

"You're late, Kyon! You too, Koizumi! What were you doing? We're running on a deadline here! If we don't hurry, we're gonna be in trouble!"

This wasn't the first time I'd seen her so happy. This is how Haruhi always looks when she's gotten her eyes fixed on a goal.

"We've been going crazy searching for the old newsletters the literature club put out. I asked Yuki where they were, but she said she didn't know."

Nagato was plopped down at her usual corner of the table, staring at the screen of the laptop the computer club had left us.

"Um…" Asahina stood there, fidgeting uncomfortably in her maid outfit. "Are we making a book? Do we have to? What are we going to write, I wonder…?"

I hadn't forgotten about this either. Haruhi had swallowed the president's story about the literature club's job of printing a whole newsletter. It was for Nagato's sake. Nagato was the sole member of the literature club, and in reality she had another face as a member of an unauthorized student organization that occupied the literature club's room. Said unauthorized organization's chief had agreed to create a publication, which by the principle of commutative responsibility now fell upon my head, and for a publication to exist in the first place, someone would have to write something, and that "someone" would have to be me and the other club members.

"All right, pick one."

Four folded scraps of paper lay in the open palm of Haruhi's hand—the same kind of lots used to determine classroom seating assignments. Doubting what these scraps could possibly decide, I picked one up. Haruhi immediately grinned.

Koizumi amusedly did likewise, as did Asahina, who blinked rapidly. Haruhi gave the last scrap to Nagato.

"You will write what is written on the paper. That will go into our club newsletter. Now that it's decided, hurry and sit down! You've got to get to writing!"

An unpleasant premonition ran though my body as I opened the piece of folded notebook paper. Haruhi's writing leaped up at me like a freshly landed fish.

"A love story." I read the contents aloud and immediately bemoaned my fate. A love story? *Me?* That was what I had to write? I asked.

"Yup." Haruhi grinned like a cunning tactician who took advantage of every weakness. "The lottery decided it fair and square. I shall brook no complaints. So, what're you doing, Kyon? Get your butt in front of the computer!"

I looked and saw several laptops set up on the table. It was nice that she hadn't had trouble getting everything set up, but how the hell was I supposed to write a story just because she told me to?

The paper in my hand felt like a grenade whose pin had been pulled out.

"What'd you get, Koizumi?" I asked, hoping that he'd be willing to switch with me, thereby securing my salvation, but—

"It says…'Mystery,'" said Koizumi with a pleasant smile, not looking particularly troubled at all. Asahina, however, was upset, as usual.

"I got 'Fairy Tale.' A fairy tale is for children, right? A story that's good for, um, putting children to bed? Is that right?"

47

I didn't have an answer for her. But anyway—a mystery and a fairy tale, eh? Between those and a love story, which one was the best?

I looked to Nagato. She'd quietly opened her scrap of paper, and upon noticing my gaze, showed me Haruhi's handwriting with a flick of her wrist. The writing read: "Fantasy Horror."

I didn't really understand the difference between fantasy horror and mystery.

"I'm just relieved I didn't get 'love story.' I feel as though such a thing would've been impossible for me to write," said Koizumi, as though he were trying to deliberately get on my nerves. He was obviously calm. I wanted to know the secret behind his relaxed attitude, I said.

"It's quite simple. In my case, I can simply treat the mystery games from last summer and this last winter as real events and create a novelization of them. They are originally scenarios I created, after all."

Koizumi coolly headed for the table and began setting up his computer, looking totally unconcerned. Nagato returned her gaze to the liquid crystal display in front of her, unmoving. She might have been considering what "fantasy horror" meant, or thinking about Kimidori.

There was no further explanation. Asahina's eyes practically projected question marks around the room as she flailed around, at a loss. I was no different. Wait—let's think about this. There were four scraps of paper. The SOS Brigade has five members.

"Haruhi," I said to the brigade chief, who was grinning like a temple guardian on laughing gas. "What are *you* going to write?"

"Oh, I'll write something," she said as she sat at her desk and picked up the armband that had been left there. "But I have a more important job. Listen—there's a lot of work that goes into making a book. You need a person to direct it all. And that's what I'm gonna do for you."

She quickly slipped on the armband, puffing out her chest and speaking grandly.

"Starting today and for the rest of the week, I will no longer be the brigade chief. Since this is the literature club, there's a different title that's much more appropriate."

The brilliantly shining armband said all that was necessary.

Thus it was that Haruhi appointed herself as editor in chief, boldly declaring her intentions as she utterly ignored Asahina's and my bewilderment.

"Come now, everybody! Get moving! There's no use complaining about details—just write! Something good, of course."

Haruhi reclined arrogantly in her brigade chief's chair and regarded us pitiful brigade members.

"And of course, if I don't think it's good, then it's out."

And so—

In the week that followed, we were stationed in the literature club's room, toiling away at this suddenly literature-club-like activity.

It was Asahina who ran bravely at the fore. It was fortunate that fairy tales seemed to suit her, but if writing one was a simple matter of sitting down and cranking it out on command, then anybody could be a fairy-tale author.

Nevertheless, Asahina was persistent. She checked out a pile of books from the school library and read through them with utmost seriousness, occasionally flagging sections with Post-it notes, scribbling furiously with her pencil.

Meanwhile there was Haruhi, whose main job seemed to be either grinning maniacally as she gazed at the many fanzines she'd borrowed from the manga club for the purpose of study material, or aimlessly browsing the Net on her desk's computer.

Asahina steadily submitted manuscripts, and Haruhi steadily rejected them.

"Hmm." Haruhi managed a plausible sound of ambivalence as she finished reading the exhausted Asahina's latest effort. "It's getting better, but it still needs more impact. Oh, I've got it, Mikuru! You need to add some illustrations. Make it like a picture book. It'll draw people in more quickly, and give it more flavor than just plain old words."

"P-pictures?"

Asahina looked ready to cry at this latest and totally unreasonable demand. But rejecting the orders of the editor in chief was no easy task, so Asahina resigned herself to adding illustrations.

The always serious girl attended a lecture on sketching given by the art club, learned four-panel comic creation from the manga club, and worked so hard that it made me want to tell her there was no need to go to such lengths—and with no time left over for her to brew good tea, I was left to idly, silently sip mediocre tea brewed by either myself or Koizumi.

And I had to write a love story, of all things? No way. If it'd been a feline observation diary, I would've had material aplenty, but...

The only one of us making easy progress on his composition was Koizumi; even Nagato only occasionally hit a key. When it had come to a video-game contest, her fingers had flown over the keyboard with unbelievable speed, but evidently she didn't have the knack for putting the information in her head into words. I was starting to wonder if that was part of why she tended to be so silent, but I couldn't help but be interested in the "fantasy horror" story she was writing, so I snuck a glance at the display of her laptop.

"..."

Nagato quickly rotated the laptop sideways, hiding the display from me. She looked up at me.

"C'mon," I said. "Let me have a bit of a look."

"No," replied Nagato flatly. No matter how I tried to sneak a look, her timing in moving the display away from me was perfect. I was starting to get more and more interested, and eventually tried sneaking up and looking over her shoulder, but besting Nagato's reflexes was impossible.

"..."

Finally she repelled me with a sharp sidelong glare. I returned to my own seat to confront the blank white screen of my empty word-processor document.

Thus had the past few days in the clubroom unfolded.

Things had begun to reach a bit of a stalemate, so while it might be technically a false start, let's go for a change of pace and have a look at Asahina's fairy tale.

Asahina's manuscript had been rejected over and over by the editor in chief, who'd eventually ordered her to add illustrations, and Asahina had continued to agonize over the piece, killing herself over every word selection. I'd finally come to her aid, and the work had eventually been completed once the editor in chief added her own revisions.

Anyway, feel free to have a look.

1

It was not so very long ago, though this story did happen in the past.

Deep in the forest of a certain country, there was a small cottage.

In that cottage lived Snow White and seven dwarves.

This Snow White had not been chased out of her home, but rather had run away from the castle of her own free will. Apparently life in the castle was not very much fun. Though it was a small country, she was a princess, and would thus eventually be forced into a political marriage of convenience. Quite distasteful, don't you think? Snow White thought so too.

But soon she began to get bored with life in the forest.

Thanks to the seven dwarves, Snow White didn't have to worry about the basic necessities, and she got along very well with all the animals of the forest, but she had begun to wonder if life in the castle might not have been quite so bad.

Though she'd selfishly run away, everyone in the castle was a nice person. The political marriage simply could not be helped. In an age of rival warlords, the only way for a small nation to survive was to give a hostage to a stronger nation in order to cement an alliance.

## 2

At the same time, a mermaid swimming in an ocean near that very same forest saved a prince who'd been thrown from his ship in a shipwreck.

The mermaid carried the prince to shore, and the prince remained unconscious the entire time. No matter what she did, he stayed asleep. The troubled mermaid decided to take the prince to Snow White's cottage.

Snow White and the mermaid had been friends ever since Snow White's arrival in the forest. The mermaid remembered Snow White's instructions: "If you ever find anything interesting, you should bring it to me."

After asking a kind witch to change her tail fins into legs, the mermaid carried the unconscious prince to the dwarves' cottage.

Even upon seeing the prince the mermaid had brought her, Snow White was not especially pleased. He wasn't exactly what she'd had in mind when she said "anything interesting."

Nevertheless, caring for the unconscious prince was amusing enough at first, although as time went on it became more and more tiresome. He simply wouldn't wake up. She had gotten sick of looking at his sleeping face.

Just as she was beginning to wonder if a good hard slap would awaken him, a messenger from the castle arrived for Snow White.

The messenger told her that the neighboring empire had suddenly mobilized its armies and had crossed the border, surrounding the castle, and its fall was not far in the future—indeed, it may have already fallen.

Things were bad.

### 3

Having heard this, Snow White left the prince—who wouldn't wake up no matter how long she waited—in the care of the mermaid, and she left the forest, along with the seven dwarves. The first place they went was a steep and craggy mountain. There lived a cunning military tactician who had given up worldly ways and become a hermit. Normally he refused to associate with anyone unless he or she visited him three times, but Snow White ordered the dwarves to capture him, and she appointed him her chief of staff. The tactician gave a pained smile; said, "Sure, why not"; and swore loyalty to Snow White.

Once Snow White's procession, now nine people strong, had descended the mountain, they began to gather volunteer soldiers at the towns and villages the imperial army had not yet reached. It was far from the number needed to defeat the empire's military forces, but Snow White still raised an anti-imperial flag and set her eye upon the castle. Her followers defeated imperial ambush forces one by one, winning a series of victories in various locations, whereupon she recaptured the castle, pursued and eliminated the retreating imperial forces, then continued her reversal of the invasion and toppled the empire, making it a part of her own domain. What a surprise.

But that was not the end. Snow White, the seven dwarves, and the tactician all assembled a great army and swept across the land, and through a variety of strategies and intrigues, they united the continent. The age of warring states came to an end, and peace reigned.

4

Snow White, who now had nothing to do, decided to leave the details to the tactician and return to the forest. Though her worries about an arranged political marriage were no more, life at the castle was boring. She preferred being able to play on her own in the forest.

Snow White, along with the seven dwarves, returned to the cottage, and they were all surprised to find that the prince was still sleeping. She had forgotten all about him.

Oh, the mermaid had taken care of him in the meantime.

Grabbing an apple that a visiting bear had brought with him, Snow White used it to whack the prince on the head.

"How much longer are you going to sleep? Wake up!"

It is said that three days later, the prince opened his eyes.

As to what happened after that, no one knows.

But I'm sure that everyone lived happily ever after. I think that would be nice.

＊　＊　＊

…How shall I put it—it was very Asahina-like, an allegorical tale that was a jumble of fairy tales and war stories. More than anything else, the sense of desperation in it was very clear. It was surely adequate. As to which parts were the results of Haruhi's meddling, I'll leave that to your imagination.

Now, then, enough about Asahina's worries—my real problem was that I still hadn't touched my own assignment. Just asking me to write a story of any kind was unreasonable enough; making it a *love* story went right past "unreasonable" into the universe of totally foreign experiences. What could I possibly do?

On the other hand, Haruhi was engaging in surprisingly editor-like activities.

Haruhi asserted that the number of pages the four of us had produced was insufficient, and moreover lacked variety, and she resorted to recruiting outside writers.

Her first victims were Taniguchi and Kunikida, then Tsuruya and the computer club president, all of whom were given deadlines that Haruhi had determined.

By Haruhi logic they were auxiliary brigade members, despite their being totally unrelated to the literature club.

But I had no time to be sympathetic to their plight—quite the contrary, I would've been much happier if my own writing responsibility had just disappeared. Although I doubted Haruhi would tolerate such literary laziness.

The deadline set for us by the evil student council president drew nearer. One morning while waiting for the morning homeroom period to start, my ears were assaulted by the sound of Taniguchi's bitter grumbling ("Why the hell do I have to write 'a fascinating slice-of-life essay' in the first place?") and Kunikida's easygoing reply ("C'mon, that's not as bad as the 'twelve-subject study-guide column' I've got to write").

Haruhi had gotten to school later than me that day. She

thrust a sheet of copier paper at me without so much as a "good morning."

"What's this?"

"The manuscript Yuki turned in before she went home yesterday." Haruhi made a face as though she'd swallowed a filling while brushing her teeth. "I gave it a good read after I got home. It's kind of a weird story. It's got a fantasy feel to it, and I guess you could call it horror. I'm not sure what to make of it. Lengthwise, it's barely a short story. Here, read it."

I was interested in reading anything Nagato wrote, whether or not Haruhi ordered me to.

I took the paper from Haruhi, and my eyes began following the text printed upon it.

"Untitled 1"

Yuki Nagato

It was XXXX ago that I met a girl who said she was a ghost.

I asked her name. "I have no name," she answered. "Because I have no name, I am a ghost. You are the same as me, aren't you?" she said, smiling.

It was true. I was also a ghost. A being who was able to speak with ghosts was also a ghost. As I am now. But I knew that I was once named Yuki, a name that sounded like snow.

"Now then, shall we go?" she said, and I went with her. Her stride was fast, and she seemed like she was alive. "We can go anywhere. Where is it that you would like to go?"

I thought about it for a while. Where was I trying to go? Where was I? Why was I here?

But all I could do as I stood there was look into her dark eyes.

"Weren't you thinking of going to XXXX?"

It was she who finally answered. When I heard her words, I finally understood my purpose. Yes. That was where I was trying to go. Why had I forgotten? Why had I forgotten such an important role, the very reason for my existence?

It was something I should never have forgotten.

"Well, that's settled then."

The girl smiled happily. I nodded and said my thanks.

"Good-bye."

The girl disappeared, and I remained. Perhaps she had returned to where she belonged. Just as I was trying to return to where I belonged.

Something white began falling from the sky. Small, unstable water crystals. They disappeared as soon as they contacted the ground.

They were one of the wonders that fill all of space-time. This world is overflowing with wonders. I stood there, still. The passage of time lost all meaning.

That wondrous stuff continued to fall, piling up like cotton.

I decided to give it my name.

So I thought, and in thinking so, I became a ghost no longer.

*　　*　　*

"Bwuh...?" I got that far before looking up.

I was greeted by the familiar sight of my fellow students filing into the classroom before the morning homeroom period started. If this had been a usual morning, Haruhi would've been sitting behind me either gazing out the window or poking me in the back with a mechanical pencil, but *this* morning she was craning her neck to peer over my shoulder, her eyes following the letters of the manuscript I held in my hands, her expression at once thoughtful and troubled.

To be fair, my own expression wasn't all that different from hers.

Both of our expressions were thanks to what was written there. It was a little heavy to be reading first thing in the morning.

It was true that the paper Nagato had drawn said, "Fantasy horror."

I moved my eyes from Nagato's writing and regarded Haruhi's profile.

"Hey, Haruhi, I'm not exactly an expert on either fantasy or horror, but is this what fantasy horror looks like these days?"

"Beats me." Haruhi put her hand to her chin, cocking her head just like an editor agonizing over how to judge a piece of work in front of her. "I guess there's some fantasy there, but there's definitely no horror. But... hmm. It does seem very Yuki-like. Maybe Yuki finds this kind of thing scary."

Anything that would scare Nagato surely would utterly terrify me. I didn't want to ever experience anything like that—not even in a story.

"Hey, by the way," I said, looking at Haruhi's confused face as a new thought occurred to me. "If you didn't know what 'fantasy horror' was, why did you write it down on one of the lots? You've got to think before you pick genres like that."

"I did think! A little." Haruhi took the manuscript sheet out of my hands. "I added fantasy to it because I thought horror by itself wouldn't be much fun. The genres I wrote down were the result of serious deliberation. Mystery, fairy tale, love story—once you've done those, you've gotta go with horror."

She'd skipped science fiction entirely. And anyway, I seriously doubted she'd spent more than three seconds picking out those genres. I bet she'd just written them down in whatever random order they'd occurred to her, I said.

Haruhi smiled slightly. "I just wanted to mismatch the writing projects as much as I could. Yuki'd probably be great at science fiction, but that wouldn't be any fun, would it?"

I twitched involuntarily, but an invisible hand calmed my hammering chest. Whether or not it would actually be "fiction," it would be the easiest thing in the world for Nagato to write something about space. I mean, she was a space alien. For a moment I wondered if Haruhi had realized that, but then I remembered—even Haruhi could see that Nagato's bookshelves overflowed with SF, so it wasn't much of a stretch to assume that science fiction was a specialty of hers.

No, wait a sec. If that were true, then there'd be a similar setup for the mystery genre, I said.

"That's right. I really hoped either you or Mikuru would do the mystery. I wanted to see what kind of crazy thing you'd come up with. But with science fiction, you can pretty much get away with any kind of absurdity—so while it pained me to do it, I had to cross it off the list."

I wanted to tell her that was just her prejudice talking, but no amount of complaining about the lottery was going to reset time. The order with which I'd been burdened—writing a love story— wasn't going to be rescinded, and I didn't feel much *more* capable of writing mystery, fairy tale, or fantasy horror stories—not that I'm saying I preferred the love story, mind you. But at least with science fiction, I could've used some of my experiences as a foundation. Although I probably had no business informing editor in chief Haruhi about my true-life experiences.

Haruhi flipped through Nagato's fantasy horror short story. "At least Koizumi got the mystery. If we don't get at least one readable story, we won't be able to put out a newsletter. If all we do is show off how eccentric we are, the readers will head for the hills."

She was already thinking about turning the literature club newsletter into a periodical. This was supposed to be an emergency measure to stop the student council president's evil plot. That was probably something I had to remind her about. The SOS Brigade was not part and parcel with the literature club; it was just a parasite, I told her.

"I know that much. I can't think of a single thing I need you to tell me about the school. I am the brigade chief, and you are just a member." Haruhi glanced at me. "Anyway, that doesn't matter. There's more to Yuki's story. Read the second page."

I dropped my gaze to the sheet of copier paper that remained in my hand and began reading the printed characters there, which were so neat I wondered if they were Nagato's handwriting.

"Untitled 2"

Yuki Nagato

Up until that point, I had not been alone. There were many of me. I was one of many.

My other selves, once bound together like ice, soon dispersed like water, then finally diffused like vapor.

One atom of that vapor was me.

I could go anywhere. I went many places and saw many things. But I learned nothing. The act of seeing was the only function I was permitted.

I performed that function for a long span. Time was meaningless. In that false universe, no illusion held any meaning.

But eventually I found meaning. Proof of existence.

Matter attracts matter. That was true and correct. It was because it possessed a shape that I was drawn in.

Light, darkness, inconsistency, sense. I met each, intersected with each. I did not have their capabilities, but I might have liked to have them.

If I were permitted to, I would have them.

As I continued to wait, would those wonders fall?

Those tiny wonders.

\*　　\*　　\*

Thus concluded the second page.

"Hrrmmm…"

I cocked my head and read it over and over. It wasn't really horror, and it was hard to call it fantasy horror—it was difficult, even, to call it a story. If it were anything, it was sort of memoirish. Or it was a simple reflection, or it was just words she'd randomly strung together.

Nagato's story, eh…?

As I was reading it, I thought of something else. Something that happened during December of last year, something I'll never forget, no matter how long I should live. That other Nagato, there in the literature club room—could she have been writing a story? All alone on that ancient computer?

I don't know how Haruhi interpreted my silence and my thoughtful face, but she snatched the paper out of my hands.

"Then there's the last page, the third one. The more you read it, the less sense it makes. I'd like to hear your thoughts."

"Untitled 3"

Nagato Yuki

There was a black coffin in the room. There was nothing else.

Atop the coffin in the middle of the room, there sat one man.

"Hello," he said to me. He smiled.

Hello.

I said the same thing to him. I don't know what my expression was.

As I continued to stand there, a white cloth floated down behind the man. In the darkness, the cloth was bathed in faint light.

"I am sorry for being late," said the white cloth.

It was actually a person, who was covered by the white cloth. There were holes cut where the eyes would be, and black pupils looked out at me.

The person within the cloth seemed to be a girl. I could tell from the voice.

The man laughed in a low voice.

"The presentation has not yet begun."

He did not move from the coffin.

"There is still time."

The presentation.

I tried to remember. Had I come here to present something? I was nervous. I could not remember.

"There is time," said the man. He smiled at me. The white sheet girl danced happily.

"Let us wait. Until you remember," said the girl. I looked at the black coffin.

I remembered only a single goal.

I belonged within that coffin.

I had come from it, and I had returned here so that I could go back to it. The man was sitting on the coffin. If he did not move, I could not get into it.

But I had nothing to present. I was not qualified to participate in the presentation.

The man began to sing in a low voice. The white sheet danced along with it.

If he did not move, I could not get into it.

* * *

"…Hmm. This is a tough one."

I laid the third page on my desk and empathized with Haruhi.

Good old Nagato had written something totally incomprehensible. She seemed to have completely ignored the fantasy-horror topic, and this was hardly a story—it was more of a poem, I said.

"It doesn't seem like just any old poem, though." Haruhi collected the three pages and put them into her bag. "Hey, Kyon. I don't think Yuki just wrote this without thinking about it. I think she's really revealing something about herself here. Don't you think all that stuff about the ghost and the coffin is a metaphor for something?"

"How the hell should I know?" I said, but the truth was that I felt like on some level I could understand it. I didn't see how the "I" in the story could be anyone besides Nagato. As for the other characters—the ghost girl, the man, and the sheet girl—I had the sense that the ghost girl and the sheet girl were the same person, and that (I was just guessing here, but…) the man was Koizumi-ish and the girl was Asahina. In any case, she'd probably used the people around her as models for the characters. Haruhi and I hadn't shown up, but I wasn't so worried about it that I wished I'd been included.

"Anyway, does it matter?" I looked out the window and down at the tennis courts. "Nagato wrote the story she wanted to write. Trying to read an author's mind through her work is a pain. That kind of question belongs on modern-literature tests."

"I guess." Haruhi also looked out the window. She seemed to be looking up at the clouds, as though willing them to bring unseasonal snow. Eventually she turned back to me and smiled like a blooming spring flower. "We'll call this okay, then. Yuki's done. There's no telling how it'd turn out if I made her rewrite it. Koizumi seems to be making steady progress, and Mikuru's getting close to finishing her illustrations." Her smile shifted from brigade chief to editor in chief. "So, what about you? I haven't even gotten so much as a prologue from you. When will it be done?"

I had been wrong to hope she had forgotten about it.

"Let me just say," began Haruhi with an unpleasant grin, "that I want a proper story from you. And if it's not a love story, it's getting spiked. Spiked! Not a horror story, or a mystery, or a fairy tale. And don't try to weasel out of it either, because it won't work."

I looked around the classroom for some sort of salvation.

The truth was that I hadn't written so much as a single word. Of course I hadn't. Why the hell did I have to write a *love* story, anyway? The question was racing through my body faster than an immune system overreacting to the influenza virus. I'd thought about trying to summon reinforcements in the form of Taniguchi and Kunikida (who themselves had also failed to write anything), but my two supposed friends had been looking over at me for some time, whispering to each other and avoiding my gaze, and just when I was about to cross myself, Catholic-style, in preparation for being crushed along with my friends by Haruhi's assault, the school bell finally rang.

I was thus able to avoid confronting the advancing burden, but that didn't mean I had escaped—I had merely bought myself some time.

But seriously, Haruhi—a *love story*?

I pretended to take the first-period class seriously, sinking deeply into thought, like a ship plunging to the bottom of the Challenger Deep.

So what was I going to write?

After school, I went to the clubroom to escape Haruhi's manuscript demands.

"What about writing something based on your personal

experience?" said Koizumi, his fingers moving swiftly over the keyboard of his laptop. "In other words, why not just get involved in a romance? Then you can simply write what happens and claim it's fiction. I recommend using first-person perspective. In such a case, it wouldn't be hard to transform your normal thoughts into prose."

"Is that your idea of sarcasm?" I shot back, before returning myself to the pressing job of staring at my own laptop's screen saver.

The clubroom had temporarily become a safe place, since Haruhi was away from her desk.

Even now she was running all over the place as part of her campaign of total war against the student council; she was so cunning that I wanted to add "demon" to the part of her armband that read "editor in chief."

Her first targets had been her nearby classmates, Taniguchi and Kunikida. No sooner had homeroom period ended than Haruhi had quickly seized the escaping Taniguchi, and with a brief exchange ("I'm going home." "I won't let you."), the battle was joined. Kunikida didn't even bother trying to escape, and soon she'd forced them into seats and put sheaves of loose-leaf paper in front of them.

"You're not leaving until you're done writing."

Her face was strangely happy, perhaps from the pleasure of having discovered a new outlet for her sadism.

Taniguchi continued to grumble, while Kunikida simply shook his head softly and picked up a pencil. He didn't seem to be too put out, but Taniguchi complained bitterly about the imposition, as though he'd realized that even minor involvement with Haruhi's machinations might cause him to someday miss the bus to paradise. I could understand where he was coming from. Unless they wrote the interesting essays that Haruhi demanded, they couldn't even dream of escape.

"What the hell is 'an interesting slice-of-life essay' supposed to be, anyway?" said Taniguchi. "Kyon, listen—slices of your life are way more interesting, anyway. You should be writing this."

No thanks. I had my own literary problems.

"Suzumiya, isn't twelve columns a bit too much?" said Kunikida, relaxed. "Surely five would be more reasonable. I'm pretty good at English, math, classics, chemistry, and physics, but I'm crap at Japanese history and civics."

If he had that many specialties, then his manuscript was the only one I was looking forward to reading. Twelve subject-specific study columns. If they were actually useful, there'd be nothing I'd want to read more.

"I'm going to come back in an hour to check on you," said Haruhi to the pair, who were the only ones remaining in the classroom. "If you're not here then…you know what'll happen, right?"

After dropping that threat, she left the classroom. Our editor in chief was a busy woman.

Nevertheless, I should add that there were people who readily accepted Haruhi's writing assignments.

One of them, it goes without saying, was Tsuruya. The upperclassman, possibly the only person as formidable as Haruhi, when abstractly asked, "So, will you write something? Anything is fine!" ended up readily giving her assent.

"Sure, when's the deadline? I'll definitely have it for you! Ha ha, this'll be fun!" she answered with a smile. I wondered what she would possibly write.

There was one other—and this was not a single person, but a group. The computer club. Now that their attempt to cheat us with their rigged video game had passed and the clubs were friendly enough that Nagato would occasionally visit them, the computer club had become like a second branch of the SOS Brigade, so our brigade chief had no trouble securing a promise

from them to write a "Game-Busting Primer! Reviews of all the latest games!" or something or other. Apparently the whole club, from the president on down, was pretty into the idea. Incidentally, I'd never played a proper computer game, so I had absolutely no interest in this.

And even so, Haruhi's work was not done. Having decided to make the newsletter's cover into something worthwhile, she hoofed it over to the art club to ask who their best artist was, then strong-armed a piece out of that person—then, having decided that a newsletter filled with nothing but text wouldn't be interesting enough, went over to the manga club and ordered some illustrations. It seemed pretty presumptuous of her, but sadly I didn't want to be any more empathetic with the inconveniences of the others than I already was, so I left Taniguchi and Kunikida in the classroom and made my way back to the clubroom.

Haruhi was not there. She was running all over the school on the aforementioned errands, and while that should've made it easy for me to relax, the act of staring at a screen saver was far from being relaxing.

"Hmm. Mmm…"

Asahina was sitting at the table, wearing (for once) her school uniform, as well as a dire expression.

At this point, she hadn't yet completed her picture-bookish illustrations, so all I could see was her leaning her head over the table as she frantically moved her pencil over the paper. I had no choice but to make my own tea.

Next to her, Nagato was maintaining her usual appearance. She was like a posed doll, sitting there with a hardback book open in front of her, giving off the sense of having completed her task.

"…"

Perhaps having decided that, having turned in three short stories, her duty was finished, Nagato had returned to her usual self.

The invisible aura that had emanated from her during the meeting with the student council was like a lie.

Speaking of lies, I can honestly confess that I'd be lying if I claimed not to have been worried about Nagato. There were a million questions I wanted to ask her—what had she been feeling that had led her to write such strange stories? Did she think nothing of showing them to Haruhi? What did they mean, anyway? Would she mind writing some annotations? But I couldn't very well ask these questions in front of Asahina and Koizumi.

I'd just have to seize the opportunity the next time we were alone.

I took my eyes off of the book-reading literature club member, who'd returned to her normal expressionless mode. There were two computers running on the table; Nagato's machine had been set aside and closed as tightly as its master's lips.

I wanted to do the same thing, if I could. The guilt of wasting the planet's precious and limited resources assaulted me, and I wanted to turn the laptop's switch to the "off" position immediately. Leaving it on would only waste more energy, and while I was turning things off, I wanted to turn off my own brain as well and go into a deep sleep.

As such thoughts ran through my head, I sighed. Koizumi spoke up.

"You need not overthink things so much. Just write things how they are."

Easy for him to say, since he could just write stuff that was already in his head. I had to think of everything from scratch. Maybe he should just tell me his own romantic experiences, I said. I'd write him a lovely tale with him as the protagonist.

"I'll pass on that, thanks." Koizumi paused his touch-typing and regarded me with an inquisitive smile. Then, in a small voice: "You really have nothing? Have you never been captive to feelings of love, or even gone out with a girl? If nothing like that has happened this first year at this school—or nothing you can write about, I suppose I should say—what about before that? In middle school?"

I looked up at the ceiling and pondered my own memories. Koizumi's voice got even quieter.

"Do you remember what I told you at the baseball game?"

He was always talking about all kinds of stuff, I said, so I couldn't be bothered to remember every detail of every line he'd spoken.

"I should think you'd remember me telling you that you were batting fourth in the order because Haruhi wished it so."

I suspiciously looked at Koizumi's gentle smile. This again, eh?

"Yes, this again. It is no coincidence that you were the one to draw 'love story.'"

I'd been plenty suspicious about the randomness of lotteries for a while now. I knew full well that you didn't have to be a master of sleight-of-hand to make them turn out the way you wanted.

I glanced at Nagato, who did not particularly seem to be eavesdropping. Asahina had her hands full with her new best friends, Mssrs. Pencil and Eraser.

"In other words, Suzumiya wants to know about your past romantic history. That's why you got the love story genre. The fact that the assignment wasn't a 'memoir of your romantic experience' is proof that Suzumiya herself is a bit hesitant."

I didn't think there was a hesitant thing about her, I said. She always came barging straight in to whatever she did, without any restraint or even so much as a "Hi, how are you."

Koizumi smiled thinly. "I am speaking of her heart. Despite her exterior, Suzumiya is well aware of where that fine line is drawn. It may be an unconscious sense, which would make it all the more impressive for its keenness. In reality, she has never once done anything that would trample on any one of our hearts. Certainly not to me, anyway. On the other hand, I've only briefly been allowed to enter Suzumiya's psyche."

Come to think of it, I'd only been there twice myself. "I'm still convinced she's a girl without any sense of restraint, though," I finally managed to reply. "Otherwise, she wouldn't be able to do stuff like kicking the student council door open or hijacking the literature club. Or making me write crap like this, to be honest."

"And so what if she is? It's fun in its own way, is it not? The few students of an underdog club, going up against the might of the student council..." Koizumi's pleasant gaze grew unpleasantly distant for a moment, but he soon regained his smile. "To be honest, I dreamed of having a school life like this. More and more, I acknowledge Suzumiya as a god, and I feel I want to worship her—because she's made my dream come true."

More like he was acting in his own play, I said. Dream come true, my ass—he was pulling the strings from behind the scenes. I'd acknowledge his effort, but that was all.

"Ah, but I would never try to manipulate which assignment you drew. Let's get back to the real subject. To put it simply, Suzumiya wants you to write something about your views on love. And incidentally, I may as well say that I do as well." Koizumi's voice got a bit louder. "From what I've heard, there was a girl you got along quite well with in middle school. What about writing something about that episode?"

How many times did I have to say it? That wasn't that kind of story.

I furrowed my brow and massaged my temples, sneaking a look at the faces of the other two occupants of the room.

Asahina was focusing solely on the completion of her illustrated fairy tale, and it didn't seem like a word of our conversation had reached her ears.

As for Nagato—

She, too, seemed to be wholly concentrating on reading her book, but while I had no way of knowing how sensitive her ears were, I had my doubts as to whether it was possible to speak so quietly that she couldn't hear.

Anyway, why was I assaulted by this guilty feeling? Why had Kunikida, Nakagawa, and the rest of my middle school classmates all come to this mistaken conclusion? It was a mystery.

"I have no intention of writing that story," I said flatly. Particularly not for the satisfaction of anyone's curiosity, and *definitely* not for this smiley-eyed jerk, and—hey, what was up with that "yes, yes, I know" look in his eye? He had it all wrong, I told him. It's not because it was some memory from my past that I didn't want to think about. The whole story really just didn't matter.

"We shall leave it at that, then," said Koizumi irritatingly, then he moved on immediately to a new suggestion. "In which case, you'll need to quickly think of a different memory that you can write about. Surely you must have one. A date you went on with someone, or a time when someone admitted they had a crush on you."

Like hell I did.

My mouth was half opened in the process of telling him so when I stopped. Koizumi noticed and smiled widely. "Ah, so you do! See, there you are. Both Suzumiya and I look forward to hearing the story. Please do write it."

I wanted to know who'd made him the assistant editor. Didn't he need to get back to his novelization of the disappearance of Shamisen? I'd decide what to write on my own, thanks very much, I told him.

"Of course, you will be the one to decide. I'm simply an observer, or an adviser at best. Though at the moment I feel more like Suzumiya's proxy."

Koizumi shrugged, ending his conversation with me and turning his attention back to his computer.

I started to think.

*Sorry, Koizumi—you've gotten the wrong idea again.* In his imagination there might be a vision of me in a typical middle school boy-girl relationship, but although I'm not proud of it, no one has ever confessed feelings for me, nor have I to anyone else. My first crush was my older cousin, but she eloped with some worthless guy. I guess it was a little traumatic, but that was a long time ago.

No, indeed—there had been no love confessions, and definitely no dates.

I chuckled as a scene appeared on the insides of my eyelids.

It had been about a year earlier. The middle school graduation ceremony was over, and the scene was from the period just before I'd come to this school. I hadn't had the slightest inkling that my high school life was going to turn out the way it had, and I was just enjoying my last lazy spring break of middle school.

The tiny episode that had lodged in the cracks of my brain had begun when my little sister had brought the telephone receiver up to my room.

I stared at the ceiling, then sniffed and touched my finger to the laptop's trackpad.

The screen saver disappeared, replaced by the blank white of the text editor.

I sensed Koizumi grinning irritatingly next to me as I experimentally hit a key.

I was just warming up. If it got boring in the middle, I could easily just delete the whole thing.

Imagining I was panning for gold hidden in the cracks of my memory, I transmitted the sentences down to my fingers that I'd composed in my brain, and I started writing the opening.

It went something like this.

"It was the last bit of the final spring break of middle school, just before I would enter high school..."

It was the last bit of the final spring break of middle school, just before I would enter high school.

Although I had already received my middle school diploma, I was not yet a high school student, and I remember thinking that if I could, I wanted to stay this way forever.

Perhaps thanks to my mother sending me to cram school, I'd passed the entrance exams with a decent score—I was glad it hadn't been too hard. However, the truth was that when I first went to the school for the preliminary inspection before the exam, the prospect of trudging up and down that hill every day for three years wasn't a bright one. Incidentally, thanks to the way the school districts worked out, all of my friends from middle school were either going to a neighborhood public school or a far-off private academy, so like it or not, I was feeling pretty lonely.

At the time, I had not the faintest idea that as soon as school started, I'd find myself meeting a strange girl and being added to the membership of a bizarre brigade, so as I thought back over my middle school days and felt uncertain about my upcoming high school life, I was taking this all very seriously.

So it was that loneliness had taken over the greater part of my heart, so I amused myself by sleeping in until close to noon, going to farewell parties for my friends who were going on to other schools (parties that were really just video game tournaments), occasionally seeing random movies—but before long I got bored with all this, so after having a combination breakfast and lunch, I whiled away that random late-March afternoon lazing around in my room, considering just turning into a cow.

I slept, awoke, ate, and napped again. Eventually, as I lay there on my side, the sound of the house's landline ringing reached my ears.

There wasn't an extension in my room, so I just left it for my mom or sister to answer, and sure enough, soon my sister came into my room, bearing the cordless handset.

Thinking back on it, I now get the feeling that every time she comes into my room with the phone, it's the start of something weird.

However, at the risk of repeating myself, back then I was yet innocent; I had a dire lack of experience points.

"Kyon, phone!" said my sister, beaming.

"Who is it?"

"A girl!"

My sister pushed the phone at me, giggled, then twirled around and skipped merrily back out of my room. That was weird. Normally she'd hang around until I kicked her out. I wondered what had her in such a hurry. But anyway, who could be on the phone? Scrolling through my mental list of faces and trying to find a girl who seemed likely to call me, I punched the answer button on the receiver.

"Hello?"

After a moment, there came, "...Yes, hello. Um..."

It was definitely a girl's voice. But my search mode hadn't completed yet, so I didn't know who it was. It did seem familiar, though.

"It's me, Miyoko Yoshimura. Is this a good time? If you're busy..."

"Oh—"

Miyoko Yoshimura? Who was that?

I began to think about it as the scrolling in my head came to a stop. Now I knew why the voice sounded familiar— I'd met her many times. Her use of her full name had tripped me up. Miyoko Yoshimura's nickname was "Miyokichi."

"Oh, right. No, I'm not busy at all. I've got nothing but time."

"Oh, good," she said, sounding relieved.

I felt dubious. What could she possibly want with me?

"Are you free tomorrow? The day after is fine too. But it has to be before

85

April starts. I'd like to borrow a bit of your time."

"Er, are you asking me?" (*1)

"Yes. I'm sorry it's so sudden. Tomorrow or the next day. Are you busy?"

"Not at all. I'm totally free both days."

"Oh, thank goodness." Her soft voice had an honesty to it that sounded like it came from the bottom of her heart. "I have a favor to ask." Miyoko continued, her voice sounding a bit nervous. "For tomorrow, just tomorrow, would you go out with me?"

I looked at my open bedroom door as if to chase the shadow of my sister. "Me?"

"Yes."

"With you?"

"Yes." She lowered her voice. "Just the two of us would be best. Will it not work out?"

"No, it's fine."

"Oh, thank goodness." She let out another exaggerated exhalation of relief, then spoke as though she were trying to contain her cheer. "Well, then, I'll see you!"

I felt like I could see her bowing at the other end of the phone line.

Next she confirmed the time and place of the rendezvous, all the while taking care that it was convenient for me. "Got it," I finally said.

"I'm sorry to have called so suddenly."

"No, it's fine. I wasn't busy," I said vaguely to this girl who was evidently determined to be considerate to the end, then hung up. I got the feeling that if I didn't hang up, there was no telling for how long Miyoko would insist on thanking me. That's just the kind of girl Miyoko "Miyokichi" Yoshimura was.

I went to return the phone receiver to its place, emerging into the hallway. There I saw my sister waiting, cackling about something. I took the opportunity to push the receiver at her.

"Nyahaha!" She giggled like a maniac, waving the receiver around in the air as she left.

Worrying about my little sister's future, I thought about the calm, reserved quality of Miyokichi's voice. (*2)

Then, the next day came.

I don't have any intention of writing all the details. To put it simply, that's because it's a pain. This is a story, not a business report or a ship's log. And it's definitely not my personal journal.

Since I'm the writer, I should be able to write whatever I like. And I think I'll do just that, thanks very much.

When I got to the rendezvous point, I saw Miyokichi's form as she walked rapidly toward me, having arrived earlier.

Once she'd realized I had seen her, she gave me a neat little bow.

"Good morning," she said in a slight voice, arranging her small purse's strap on her shoulder and looking up at me, the movement of which caused her braid to sway a bit. She had a pale blue cardigan on over a floral-patterned blouse, along with fitted jeans. Her outfit suited her slim frame nicely.

"Hey," I said in reply, and looked slowly over the surroundings.

We were in front of the train station. It was the same location I would come to be very familiar with as the usual meeting place of the SOS Brigade. But at that time, since I had no idea that in a few short months I'd be a member of a bizarre brigade and would be constantly dragged around by a crazy brigade chief bent on world domination, it all looked pretty normal to me. If anyone saw me meeting up with a girl, they wouldn't have any reason to think anything annoying would happen. It'd never occur to you, would it? (*3)

"Um—" Miyokichi's fine features seemed a bit nervous. "There's someplace I'd like to go—would it be all right?"

"Sure." That's why I'd shown up, after all. If I hadn't planned on coming along, I would've turned her down the previous day on the phone. And there was no reason for me to refuse her request.

"Thank you." She really didn't need to be this polite, but there she was, bowing again. "There's a movie I would like to see."

Sure, no problem. I'd even buy her ticket, I said.

"There's no need for that. I'll pay for myself, since I'm the one who asked you all the way out here," she said plainly, then smiled. Is this what they mean when they say "a smile pure as the driven snow"? It was almost too innocent, though in a different way than my little sister's.

Incidentally, there were no theaters in the area. Miyokichi and I headed back to the station, bought tickets, and got on the train. The film she wanted to see wasn't playing at the big multiplex; it was a minor indie flick playing only at a small one-screen theater.

As the train swayed, she looked out the window, clutching a town guidebook in her hand. Occasionally, she would seem to remember something and look up at me, then give a quick little bow.

I wasn't totally silent myself—I made reasonable conversation, but it wasn't anything worth writing. It was just small talk. I remember talking about where we would be going to school in the spring, or what my little sister was like. (*4)

It was the same way once we arrived at our planned station and walked to the movie theater. She just seemed a little nervous. That nervousness continued all the way up to the ticket booth. (*5)

It was almost time for the next show to start, but there was no one lined up at the booth, which said something about the low attendance of the film. "Two students," I said to the bored-looking lady on the other side of the glass when she looked up at us.

*       *       *

...Having gotten this far, I took my hands off the keyboard, leaned back in the folding chair, and stretched.

I really wasn't used to doing this kind of thing, so my shoulders were unavoidably tight. As I rolled my head around to loosen my neck—

"You seem to be moving right along," said Koizumi, looking both pleased and interested. "Keep it up until the end, if you please. I truly look forward to reading whatever you write."

Too bad for you, Koizumi. I was willing to bet on it. This wasn't something that would be fun to read, I told him. It was pretty far off the mark from a love story.

"Even so," said Koizumi as he poked at the liquid-crystal display of his own laptop, "I'm intrigued by whatever you write, because writing always reveals at least a little bit about the writer. You can always hear the voice of the author speaking out between the lines. I'm interested in your writing, more than I am in Nagato's or Asahina's."

There wasn't any need for him to be interested, I told him. Since when had he taken on any job besides being an expert on Haruhi psychology? Wasn't performing psychoanalysis on me outside of his job description?

"Considering that Suzumiya's mental state is affected by yours, I don't think you can assert that unconditionally, no."

Did his impudence know no bounds?

I ended my exchange with Koizumi and looked over the room. Haruhi had yet to return, and Asahina was still drawing her pictures.

"Mmmm...hmm..." The cute upperclassman was bent over the drawing paper, a look of extreme concentration on her face as she childishly gripped a pencil, first drawing a line, then thinking for a moment, then rubbing the line out with a rubber eraser, finally *hmm*-ing again before hunching over the paper and continuing her work. Although I've already introduced you to the final product, at the time Asahina was still working on it. Given the results, her effort certainly paid off—and it turned out to be a very Asahina-like story too.

At this point, the only one of us who had finished her story was Nagato, who sat at her designated corner of the table, silently reading. Having completed her triad of untitled short stories, the sole literature club member sat and quietly read her book, ignoring Asahina and me, as well as Haruhi's delighted running around, as though we were none of her concern.

For my part, I wanted to ask for some author's notes regarding *Untitled 1*, *2*, and *3*, but I decided it would be better not to, and in any case, my main worry at that moment was the "love story" I'd been assigned. I should've been writing my brains out, but I couldn't stand the idea of turning something in only to have Haruhi say, "It's boring. Rejected."

How'd I let myself get cornered into caring so much about something I couldn't do anything about?

Just as I was letting it really get me riled up, that pleasant smile came at me again from the side.

"But that's not really so, is it?" said Koizumi, as though refuting my internal monologue. His fingers never left the keyboard as he continued touch-typing. "If you write something about a past experience, something from before you met Suzumiya and me, I'm sure she'd be very interested to read it."

I was impressed at his ability to talk and type at the same time— but his assurances didn't make me feel any better, I told him.

"For example," said Koizumi, vaguely amused, "haven't you ever wondered about my past? What I did before I transferred to this school? What I thought of as I passed my days? Have you never wanted a glimpse of that?"

Well, now...that all depends. If it were a piece of nonfiction that depicted the daily life of an esper, then my elementary-school self would be jumping for joy to read it. Even now my intellectual curiosity was piqued by the organization known as "The Agency."

"If you knew the truth, you'd only be disappointed. There aren't any particularly interesting episodes. As you yourself are aware, I am an esper whose potency is limited to a very specific time and place," said Koizumi. "However, it is true that my days do differ from the days of ordinary people. I do occasionally consider writing an autobiography, once things have calmed down. If I finish it, I'll have to put your name in the dedication."

"Don't bother."

"Oh? I would certainly want to give you a complimentary copy."

I reached out for my tea, not answering. The teacup was empty. Since Asahina was still working, I would have to get another cup on my own, which I stood to do.

*Bang.* The room's door slammed open, and in charged an energetic girl.

"Hey, everybody! Making good progress?"

Haruhi was so lively that it seemed a bit odd as she strode straight to the brigade chief's seat, sat down, put on the desk the sheaf of papers she had been holding, and turned her eerily bright gaze to me.

"Oh hey, Kyon—if you're making tea, get some for me too. Mikuru's busy and I'd feel bad interrupting her."

There was no point in childishly quibbling with her over something so trivial. I expressed my irritation with an audible sigh, then filled the teapot with hot water, poured tea into my cup as well as Haruhi's, and became a temporary waiter as I brought it to her.

Haruhi cheerfully took the cup and sipped from it. "What's this? It's just hot leaf juice. Change the tea leaves, will ya?"

"You do it. I'm busy."

It was the truth—I *was* busy, so even if the brigade chief had been thankful for the tea, a bit of mutinous behavior would be forgiven. She couldn't very well claim that tea-brewing was more important than working on the newsletter.

Haruhi grinned. "Oh, so you *are* working. Finally! I'm impressed. You better make the deadline. We're gonna have to start doing the layouts soon."

I sipped the tea I'd brewed and speculated on the cause of Haruhi's high spirits. It likely had something to do with the sheaf of A4 papers that she'd tossed onto her desk.

"Oh, this?" The ever-perceptive Haruhi noticed what I was looking at. "They're finished manuscripts. Ones I commissioned. Everybody did a pretty good job. Taniguchi insisted he couldn't write anything, so I gave him an extension until tomorrow. Kunikida was about half done. They're taking it seriously, so they'll be done tomorrow."

Humming a tune to herself, Haruhi flipped through the manuscripts page-by-page as though checking them over. "Here are the illustrations I got from the manga club, and here's the art club's rough illustration for the cover. This is the piece from the computer club. These'll buy us a few pages, at least. I've got no idea about what they wrote, but who cares? I'm sure their enthusiasm comes through, and people who know about video games will get something out of it."

Ah, so that's how it was. In essence, it seemed Haruhi had found happiness in the process of pushing the publication forward. Making something out of nothing as we gradually progressed toward completion—hell, even I thought it was pretty fun. It was sort of like gradually building a plastic model out of tiny parts or moving toward the final boss in an RPG. It was enjoyable, so long as you weren't one of the model pieces or NPCs.

"What're you mumbling about?" Haruhi polished off her tea

briskly, grinning at me as she shook the emptied cup around. "You better hurry up and get back to your seat. C'mon, write! The computer club's not even in the brigade, and look what they did! If you slack off, we'll get a reputation for being slackers. We're the ones who originally accepted this challenge, after all."

Having a worthy organizational rival seemed to energize Haruhi. It was enough to make me want to tell her the truth about the student council president, just to irritate her. The original trumped-up charge had been against Nagato as a member of the literature club, and Haruhi had simply decided to barge in and take over leadership—even going so far as to wear an editor-in-chief armband.

I glared over at Koizumi, wondering how many plans he'd dreamed of to stave off her boredom. The island mystery had definitely been the first, and the nonsense on the snowy mountain had been number two. No, wait—what about the thing with Kimidori and the cave cricket? Oh, right, that had been Nagato's doing.

I was reflecting on such nonsense when a knock suddenly sounded at the door.

"Excuse me." The door opened before anyone had time to answer it, and a tall, thin figure entered the room.

*Tinkk!*

I was probably the only one who heard the sound, like a piano wire being snipped by wire cutters.

It was like the sub-boss of a shooter had appeared: there he was, the student council president.

The president's glasses reflected meaninglessly, indicating he was in serious business mode. He swept his gaze slowly over the room.

"This is quite a nice room. I'm even more convinced it's wasted on the likes of you."

"What're you doing here? You're interrupting our work—just

get lost." Haruhi flipped into irritated mode faster than a super-hero changing costume. She crossed her arms, looking even haughtier than the president, not even bothering to stand up.

The president calmly endured her murderous gaze. "Think of it as enemy reconnaissance. I have no intention of being your constant foe or an obstacle you must overcome. I came only to check up on you, as is my responsibility. Think of it as a checkup to make sure you're being serious. From what I can tell, you're certainly flailing around quite a bit. That's all well and good, but movement does not necessarily translate into results. Let us say that you must continue devoting yourself to the task."

It wasn't like we needed him to come and tell us that—but before I could respond, the brigade chief (or should I say the edi-tor in chief) beat me to it.

"Shut up."

*Zing.* It was as though I could hear the sound of Haruhi's eyes turning into daggers.

"If you came just to needle us, you're out of luck. I'm not going to fall for such a clumsy jab."

"And I've no such free time." The president snapped his fingers pretentiously. I practically expected him to call out, "*Garçon,*" but the slick head of the student council was not calling for a waiter. "Kimidori, if you please."

"Yes, Mr. President."

Kimidori, holding a stack of booklets in her arms, quietly approached Haruhi.

Nagato returned her eyes to the open hardcover book in front of her, unmoving.

"..."

Kimidori smiled, giving no indication that she'd noticed Nagato. "Here you are. Reference materials." She presented the stack of musty old booklets to Haruhi.

"What're these?"

Haruhi didn't bother to hide the look of irritation on her face, her eyebrows going up as she accepted the stack like it was a cursed item of some kind.

The president adjusted his glasses sarcastically. "They're newsletters produced by previous incarnations of the literature club. Feel free to refer to them. Given your tendency toward fanciful theories, there is a distinct possibility that you're misunderstanding what constitutes 'literature.' No need to thank me. If you feel any obligation, direct it to Miss Kimidori. It was she who took the trouble to find them in the archive room."

"Huh. Thanks. Not that I'm really pleased."

Haruhi made a face like a feudal lord who'd received tribute in salt despite not particularly having a salt shortage. She dropped the booklets unceremoniously on the desk, then, as though realizing who this messenger's face reminded her of—

"Hey, you...so you got on the student council, did you?"

"Yes, starting this year," replied Kimidori politely, bowing and returning quietly to the president's side.

"Did you work things out with your boyfriend?" Haruhi asked as though she didn't really care.

"I really appreciated your help," said Kimidori, her placid smile unwavering. "But we've broken up. When I think about it now, it is as though we were never really going out together. It's a distant memory."

It was a roundabout answer, but I felt like I knew the reason. I bet the computer club prez would agree with me. He'd have no memory of any dating at all. He'd just been punished for daring to look at the SOS Brigade's website. I felt a little bad for him.

"..."

Nagato turned a page of her book.

At this point it felt like Nagato and Kimidori were engaged in a fierce battle to see who could ignore the other more. But since Nagato acted like this pretty much no matter who was around,

the battle was probably all in my head. I felt like I was wearing glasses with weird-colored lenses.

"Huh, is that so?" Haruhi curled the corners of her lips strangely. "Well, you're still young. Things happen."

In point of fact, Haruhi was even younger, but I had no intention of taking such a cheap shot. Ignorance was the key here. And in any case, Kimidori's actual age was probably the same as Nagato's. Her seniority was doubtful. I bet she'd just happened to be enrolled as a junior.

Not that I could very well say anything about that. Going by Nagato's reaction, Kimidori was not an enemy. I glanced casually over at Asahina out of the corner of my eye. At the very least, she knew that Nagato was an alien. Her shock when she was first dragged to the clubroom was proof enough of that. So my concern that she might also know the truth about Kimidori was entirely founded.

Still—

"Hmm. Oh, ah—mmm."

Thanks to the intensity of her picture-drawing efforts, the lovely upperclassman seemed not to have noticed the two intruders in the room. I wasn't sure whether to applaud her intense concentration or worry about how close she was getting to that klutzy-girl stereotype. If the latter were true, it was the result of Haruhi's training of her.

As I stood there dumbly, Haruhi and the president continued their verbal combat.

"It seems you're doing a fiction anthology," said the president nihilistically. "But are any of you even capable of writing a proper story?"

"I'll say it again: sucks to be you," Haruhi shot back. "I'm not the least bit worried."

Her face brimmed with confidence; I wanted to know what wormhole that confidence had sprung from.

She continued. "We don't need anyone to teach us. Writing a story is easy. Even this idiot Kyon can do it. Most people know how to read and write, don't they? If you can write letters, then you can write sentences, and all you have to do is connect those sentences. It's not like you need special training to learn how to write. We're high school students. We don't have to practice writing stories! We can just *write them*."

The president pushed up his glasses. "I can't help but be impressed by your optimistic outlook. It is, however, infantile."

I totally agreed, but I wished he would refrain from provoking Haruhi any further. Even if her ire were directed solely at the president, all of us in the room would have to endure her burning aura.

As expected, the angle between Haruhi's eyebrows and eyes became sharply acute. "You think you're a real big shot, huh? Well, even if you are, I *hate* big shots! And I hate small-fry people who *think* they're big shots even more!"

She certainly wasn't under-equipped for a war of words. I wondered for how long they'd keep up this performance. After all, the president *did* outrank Haruhi. It might have been just another act, but the ability to stay cool in the face of Haruhi's blazing anger was impressive. The president was pulling it off, as was Kimidori.

"Hmph. I am not particularly important. You judge people by their rank, do you? If I have anything to boast of, it is having gained my position through a legitimate public election. And how is it you've come to sit in your seat there? What was it again? 'Brigade chief'?"

I had to admit that Koizumi's choice of personnel was impressive. The president had real guts. There probably wasn't a single other student in the whole school who could face down Haruhi with such vicious sarcasm.

But Haruhi was a force to be reckoned with herself. I knew that all too well.

"There's no point in trying to provoke me," said the leader of this unauthorized student organization. "The student council may want to destroy the SOS Brigade along with the literature club, but it won't work."

Haruhi glanced at me briefly. What the hell was she looking at?

Her flashing eyes turned quickly and sharply back to the president.

"I am absolutely not moving from this spot. Want to know why?"

"I'd love to," said the president.

If Haruhi's words had been microwave radiation, then the volume she spoke at would've been more potent than any microwave oven.

"Because this is the SOS Brigade's room, and I am the chief of that brigade!"

Having said what he'd come to say and let Haruhi speak her piece, the president and his attendant left.

"Argh, so irritating! What did that idiot president come here to do, anyway?" Haruhi grumbled, her lip curled in a sneer as she flipped through the old literature club booklets that Kimidori had left.

Haruhi's war cry had finally gotten Asahina to realize that guests had entered the clubroom, but by the time she had, in a panic, started to make tea for them, it was too late—but thanks to her haste, I was able to finally enjoy her delicious tea and apply myself to my own writing... Well, no, not that last part.

Somehow, now that the mood had been wrecked, my motivation was gone. The fact that my theme had been chosen by lottery didn't help; neither did the fact that I was trying to write an episode out of my past.

But that wasn't going to be good enough. Thanks to the president's visit, Haruhi's zeal had been enflamed, and it seemed ready to blacken the ceiling with its intensity.

"Listen up, everyone." Haruhi pursed her lips before opening her mouth to speak. "It's come to this. We're going to make this newsletter if it kills us, and it's going to be great. We're not going to have a single copy left over, and we're gonna take down the president. Got that?"

The newsletter wasn't going to be sold; it was going to be given away, and furthermore I had no interest in dying for this particular cause—but I had a feeling that if I missed the deadline, whatever punishment Haruhi dreamed up would make me *wish* I were dead. I knew that it was all part of his act, but did that president really have to go this far? Ditto, Koizumi—this was no time for his self-satisfied smile.

"For my part," whispered Koizumi, right on cue, "I am extremely satisfied. So long as Suzumiya's attention is turned toward ordinary activities, I can stay away from Closed Space."

That might be good for him. But what about me? I really didn't want to get tangled up in intrigues with the student council. I understood that the president was just playing a part, but *Haruhi* didn't know that, and there was no telling what she'd resort to. If our newsletter didn't live up to the president's standards, I knew for a fact Haruhi wouldn't just turn over the clubroom to him. I definitely didn't want to wind up on the receiving end of a siege, being starved out of our castle, I told Koizumi.

He chuckled. "You're overthinking things. What we need to focus on now is finishing the publication. The rest will fall into place. If it doesn't"—a cunning expression flashed across his smiling face—"we'll simply put a different scenario into play. Starvation tactics, eh? That might do nicely."

Tsuruya had compared the student council president to the

general Sima Yi; I wondered whom she'd compare Koizumi to. Maybe the warlord Kanbei Kuroda?

I was starting to feel like the lord of Takamatsu Castle after its water supply had been cut off, and I prayed that Koizumi didn't indulge his taste for school intrigues too much.

It turned out that I wasn't able to finish my manuscript that day. After being interrupted by the president, I didn't write another word.

Fortunately, once Haruhi finished checking the pieces that had been finished, she rushed out of the room. Had she hit upon another outside source for material, or had she just gone off to deliver more "motivation"?

She returned just as the chime signaling the end of the school day rang; at the same moment, Nagato closed her book. Koizumi had made steady progress, and Asahina had put forth admirable effort. I grabbed my bag and stood.

Surprisingly, Haruhi didn't suggest I take the laptop home and continue working on it. She might have merely forgotten to be angry, but in any case, I was grateful for it.

We all left school together, and as the chilly wind came down from the mountain, it nonetheless felt like a breath of spring air, and as I made my way home, I wondered idly what would happen if a new student appeared, wanting to join the literature club. Would they be automatically drafted into the SOS Brigade?

I continued my autobiographical story the next day, after classes were over.

Let's see, how far had I gotten? Ah, that's right—we'd just bought the movie tickets.

We'll pick up from there.

Having successfully entered the theater, Miyokichi and I proceeded to seats in the middle of the theater, which was hardly what you'd call spacious. It was mostly empty, with only a scattering of other moviegoers; perhaps attendance was poor.

As for what kind of film it was—turned out it was a gory splatter-fest horror flick. To be honest, it's not really my favorite genre, but on that particular day I couldn't very well not go along with her wishes. Still, it didn't really suit her demure appearance. She must have really wanted to see this film.

During the film, she became a genuine cinema fan, eyes riveted to the screen, but she occasionally flinched and turned away in response to the startling moments you see in every horror film. Once she even grabbed my arm, which calmed me down—I don't know why.

Other than that, though, she drank the film in, every bit as focused on it as I'm sure the director would have hoped. If you want to know my impressions of the film, all I can say is that it seemed like a pretty standard B-movie. I didn't feel particularly disappointed by it, nor particularly enriched. I didn't have any memory of reading any advance reviews either. There must've been hardly any publicity.

I wondered why she'd picked this film.

When I asked, she answered, "It has my favorite actor in it," a little embarrassed.

The curtain lowered before the end credits had finished scrolling, and we left the theater.

It was afternoon. Were we going to get lunch somewhere? Was it time to go home? My musing was interrupted by her reserved, quiet voice.

"There's a shop I'd like to go to, if you don't mind. Is it all right?"

I looked to see that she was holding her city guidebook open; one of the page's corners was circled with a red pen. It was a shop that we could walk to from where we were.

I thought about it for a second. "Of course, it's fine," I answered, and we walked along the route described by the simple map. She walked diagonally behind me, quiet as ever. We must have had some sort of conversation, but I don't remember what it was.

After walking for a while, we came to our destination—a cozy little café. It was stylish outside and in, the kind of place it would take enormous guts for a guy to enter on his own, lest he feel deeply out of place. I couldn't help but stop short in front of the café, but Miyokichi's worried look was all it took to get me to push open the door like I belonged there.

As I expected, nearly all of the customers within the café were female. It was quite pleasant. There were a handful of couples, which somehow came as a relief.

The waitress led us to our table with a friendly smile, brought us ice water with a friendly smile, and even took our order with a friendly smile.

After taking thirty seconds or so to scrutinize the menu, I ordered some Neapolitan ice cream and an iced coffee, and Miyokichi got the house special cake set. She seemed to have known what she was going to order ahead of time, and from the ten varieties of cake samples the waitress brought over, she chose the Mont Blanc without any hesitation.

"You're okay with just the cake set?" I think I asked. "You won't be hungry?"

"No, I'll be fine." She straightened and put her hands on her knees, face a bit nervous. "I'm not a big eater."

It was a strange answer. She suddenly looked down, perhaps because I was gazing intently at her. I hurried to explain myself, only getting her to smile again after some effort. Now that I think about it, the embarrassing things I said are enough to make me break into a sweat. Stuff like how I thought she was perfectly lovely as she was, and...uh, yeah, I think that's all I'm going to write about that. But the truth was Miyokichi was a pretty girl—pretty enough that probably half of the boys in her class had crushes on her.

Once the food arrived, she took about thirty minutes to finish her Darjeeling tea and Mont Blanc cake. I finished first, and I had enough time left over that I'd been able to drink the water into which the ice of my iced coffee had melted.

I was getting pretty bored, but she didn't seem to have noticed, and I talked about random things with her, nodding or shaking my head as appropriate. Now that I think about it, I probably didn't have to make so much of an effort, but I was just a bundle of consideration back then. And I was pretty nervous too.

I would've been happy to pay the café tab. But she would have none of it, and she insisted on paying her own share. "I was the one who asked you out today," she said.

Having settled the bill, we walked back out into the sunlight. Where would she want to go after seeing a horror film and eating at a cute café? Or would it be time to go home?

She was quiet for a while as we walked. Then, finally—

"There is one last place I'd like to go."

She explained, in her small voice, that she wanted to come to my home.

So it was that I brought her back to my house, where my little sister seemed to be waiting for us, and the three of us all played games together.

\*    \*    \*

"Whew."

I wrote that much, then my fingers stopped.

Only Koizumi and Nagato were in the clubroom with me. Haruhi was running around like usual, and Asahina had gone to the art club for the final check on her illustrations.

I had scrolled through the entirety of the text I'd written when I saw Koizumi's face seep into the corner of my vision.

"Did you write through to the end? Already?"

"Hard to say...," I answered, but truth be told I felt like I could end it here. When I thought about it, what was the point in being so diligent about it? For the literature club's sake, and by extension for Nagato's sake—to that extent, I could see being enthusiastic, but really this was to help the SOS Brigade stay in the room and to keep Haruhi from getting bored. Koizumi was pulling the strings behind the scenes, and the president was just a guy abusing his power as Koizumi's puppet. When you got right down to it, this was one big roundabout scam.

Still, I felt like I wanted to avoid the second-stage confrontation with the student council that Koizumi was anticipating so much. Nagato was at the center of this, after all. I wanted her to be able to enjoy as peaceful a school life as possible. I wanted to believe I wasn't the only one whose heart was put at ease by seeing Nagato quietly reading her book in the corner.

"I guess this'll do." I gave Koizumi a nod. "I want to get your opinion before I show it to Haruhi. Read it, willya?"

"I'll be more than happy to."

I glanced at Koizumi's deeply interested face, then manipulated the trackpad.

The laptops in the room were networked to the desktop machine, which acted as a server. With a little bit of clicking, the printer in the corner started up and began to spit out printed pages.

*　　*　　*

Some minutes later.

Koizumi, having finished reading, smiled and offered the following comment: "I thought *I* was the one doing a mystery."

So he'd noticed, eh?

"What're you talking about?" I feigned ignorance. "I didn't try to write a mystery."

Koizumi's smile widened. "And there's another problem. Where's the love story in this?"

In that case, what did he think I'd written, I asked him.

"This is just bragging. 'I went on a date with a cute girl.' That's all."

That's what you'd normally think, yes. However, Koizumi had noticed something else, I was pretty sure. Where were his suspicions roused, I wondered?

"From the very beginning. It's rather obvious. It would be harder *not* to notice it."

Koizumi put the manuscript's pages in order, then took out a ballpoint pen and wrote marks on a few of the sheets. They were asterisks—the very asterisks you may have noticed in the manuscript yourself. He wrote those.

"You're a very considerate writer. You included a series of clues, after all. Even the most oblivious reader would have an inkling by the fourth asterisk."

I clucked my tongue, still pretending to not know what he was talking about, and glanced sideways. Seeing Nagato's unmoving figure there made me feel at ease. The sight of her did me good, but Koizumi's words were trying to corner me.

"But as it is, there's no punch line, no climax. Why not add a line or two? Just to show all your cards, so to speak. I doubt it would take much time."

Maybe I did need to add something.

I wasn't thrilled about following any advice from Koizumi, but I got the feeling that he was worth listening to this one time. Psychoanalyzing Haruhi was his specialty, after all.

But, wait a second—why should I have to worry about Haruhi's reaction? She was the one who'd gone and suggested a "love story," but *I* was the one who had to actually write the thing—the same was true for Asahina and Nagato. If we were assigning fault, it belonged with the person who'd forcibly occupied the editor in chief's seat: Haruhi.

As I stared at the liquid crystal display, Koizumi chuckled. "I doubt you have anything to worry about. If your story's meaning is something I recognize, then I very much doubt that Suzumiya will fail to do likewise. Now, before you get cross-examined... Ah, whoops—"

Koizumi reached into his blazer's pocket. There was a faint buzzing sound.

"If you'll excuse me." He pulled out his cell phone and took a look at the screen. "I seem to have some minor business to attend to. I'll be out for just a moment. No, don't worry—I just have to make a short report. It's not one of *those* cases."

With those words, Koizumi stepped out of the room, smiling all the while. I wondered if he was going to meet up with some girl on the sly. The guy was so sneaky, I wouldn't be at all surprised to find out he was somehow managing to live a normal life with none of us the wiser.

Which left only Nagato in the room, still absorbed in her book.

She did not look up. I thought about saying something, but I was still thinking about my own problem—whether or not to add those last couple of superfluous lines.

There in the silence, I closed the file that contained my pseudo-story, and I opened up a new text file. The monitor was filled with a blank white document.

Might as well write something. Like Koizumi said, just a couple of lines to end it.

My fingers clicked on the keys. The addition was short enough not to need any revision, so I just printed it out on the spot.

As I stared at the single page that emerged from the printer, I started to want to just trash the entire story. It was no good. Even given how long ago it had happened, it was too embarrassing.

I folded up that last page and slipped it into the pocket of my blazer.

Then, that moment—

"Taniguchi's run off somewhere again. I gotta get him to write something tomorrow, even if I have to tie him to the chair. Kyon, that goes for you too. If you don't finish soon, your editor in chief's gonna be mad!"

Haruhi had entered the room.

And her eyes alighted upon my manuscript, which Koizumi had left on the table.

My pleas for her to stop were in vain, as Haruhi swiftly snatched up the printout. She sat at her desk and began a leisurely read.

I was split between indignation and resignation as I watched the all-powerful editor in chief's face.

Haruhi had been grinning at first, but somewhere in the middle, her grin faded into expressionlessness. When she finished reading the last page, her expression changed again.

How strange. It was a rare thing to see Haruhi so stunned.

"This is the end?"

I nodded quietly. Nagato said nothing and continued reading the page to which her book was opened. Asahina was still out. Koizumi had left on some pretense. There was no one here who could give Haruhi any unnecessary information.

And then—

Haruhi set my manuscript on the desk, then faced me again. And then she smirked. Just like Koizumi.

"Where's the punch line?"

"What punch line?" I decided to play dumb.

Haruhi smiled beatifically; it was unsettling. "Surely you wouldn't just end it there. What happened to this Miyokichi girl?"

"I guess she went on to live happily ever after, somewhere."

"Yeah, right. C'mon, you know, don't you?"

Haruhi's hands were on the desk, but then she jumped clear over it, right at me. Before I could react, she grabbed my tie. Her ridiculous power was making it hard to breathe.

"If you want me to let you go, you better start talking. And it better be the truth."

"What do you mean, the truth? It's a story! It's fiction! The 'I' in the story isn't me; it's the first-person narrator of the story! Same for Miyokichi!"

Haruhi's smile got closer and closer as her strength constricted my throat. This was bad—I could really suffocate.

"Sure, keep lying," she said sweetly. "I never for a second believed you could write a totally made-up story. At the very least, you'd have to write something that you'd heard from somebody you knew. No, my intuition tells me that no matter how you read this, it's a true story. And it's *your* true story." Haruhi's eyes shone crazily. "Who's Miyokichi? What kind of relationship did she have with you?"

My tie constricted my throat more and more, and I finally confessed the truth.

"She sometimes comes over to my house for dinner, then goes home."

"That's all? Are you sure you're not leaving anything out?"

Reflexively, I touched the pocket of my blazer. That was enough for Haruhi.

"Ah-ha! That's where you've been hiding the rest of the manuscript, eh? Give it here."

She was way too perceptive for her own good. I couldn't help but be impressed. But before I could say so, Haruhi had resorted to force.

Haruhi thrust her right leg between my thighs and performed a perfect inside-leg trip, sumo-style. Where'd she learn that?

"Whoa," I yelled.

With Haruhi leaning on me, I fell to the floor. She straddled me like I was a horse, trying to reach into my blazer to get into the inside pocket. I tried to resist.

"Hey, knock it off!"

I looked desperately to Nagato, but when her subtle, near-expressionless gaze met mine, she too seemed to be unsure what to do.

Somewhere along the line, she had opened up her own laptop.

When had that been? She'd been able to hack into and rewrite the computer club's game program, so peeking into the contents of my laptop would be child's play for her. Had she seen it?

"..."

Nagato watched Haruhi and me wrestle on the ground, giving assistance to neither of us.

And then—

"I'm back—Wha?!"

Enter Asahina. She sure did have an incredible sense of timing. Stunned, she looked at me on the ground, with Haruhi on top of me and evidently in the midst of some kind of sexual harassment. Who knew what was going through her head?

"I-I'm sorry! I didn't see a thing, honest! Really!" she shouted, running away, having gotten the entirely wrong idea.

"..."

Nagato silently regarded us.

"So, you're not going to do as your editor in chief says? C'mon, hand it over!" Haruhi smiled wildly.

I held up my hands to defend myself as Haruhi manhandled me, a plea going out from my heart.

*Help me, Koizumi. You're my only hope. Get back here, now!*

The single sheet of paper folded up inside my blazer read as follows:

*Incidentally, Miyoko Yoshimura, also known as "Miyokichi," was my sister's best friend and classmate. At the time, she was a fourth grader in elementary school, and she was ten years old.*

*Last year, as well as now, Miyokichi was so mature-looking that it was hard to imagine she was my little sister's classmate. She was tall enough to make you doubt her claim not to be a big eater, and as far as her bearing and overall impression went, she seemed more grown-up than someone like Asahina. Thanks to that most un-elementary-school-student-like appearance, neither the box office attendant nor the ticket collector gave her a second look.*

*And even if they had noticed, it was doubtful they would have stopped her every time. After all, they'd sell you tickets at the student discount price without even checking for your student ID.*

*The film had been rated PG-12. In other words, children under twelve had to be accompanied by a guardian. I was fine, since I'd already turned fifteen.*

*The problem was Miyokichi. She knew perfectly well, however, that nobody would guess that she was younger than twelve.*

But she couldn't bring herself to go alone. Her parents were fairly strict, and they wouldn't understand a Splatterhouse B-movie—even asking them for permission to go was just begging for a lecture, she later told me.

The only friend she could really invite to go with her was my sister, who looked every inch the elementary-school student she was. The film was only going to play through the end of March. If Miyokichi didn't hurry, she'd lose her chance.

So she thought about it. Was there anyone she could go with, to whom the theater would sell tickets?

There was me.

I've always gotten along pretty well with little kids, if I do say so myself. Most of my cousins were younger than me, so I'd probably picked up the knack of playing with them after being made to watch them whenever we got together in the countryside.

Of course, dealing with my sister's friends when they came over was a common occurrence. Miyokichi was one of those friends, so she knew me well.

I was the older brother of a friend she played with often, and during the vacation I was unlikely to be busy. That was how I came to be within the circle of friends of a fourth grader.

She also considered this: if she were going to a movie, she might as well go somewhere else a kid would also have a hard time getting into. Thus she picked that café. The waitress had been very pleasant. It was too fancy for a typical elementary school student to enter on her own, and even my middle-school-age self was a little nervous to go in. If someone had spotted Miyokichi and me in there, I'm sure they would've had a hard time imagining us as anything other than brother and sister.

Miyoko Yoshimura—Miyokichi—is now a fifth grader, soon to be sixth. Give her five or so more years, and she'd be a rival for Asahina.

That is, if she ever catches Haruhi's attention somehow.

\*   \*  .  \*

Now then, the epilogue.

The newsletter was finished on time. It was printed on sheets of copier paper, stapled into booklets with a giant business-grade stapler, and the content—minus any personal bias I may have here—was pretty solid.

One particularly excellent section was the adventure story that Tsuruya wrote. The crazy piece—"Tough Luck! The Tragedy of Boy N"—had every single person who read it rolling on the floor in laughter. I myself had tears rolling down my face. It had been a long time since I was so surprised to read something so entertaining. The only one who kept a straight face while reading it was Nagato, but Tsuruya's lively slapstick comedy was so hilarious that I can easily imagine Nagato having a private chuckle, once she was alone in her own room.

I'd suspected before, but the notion came to me anew: was Tsuruya actually a genius?

As far as the other SOS Brigade affiliates went, Taniguchi wrote an impressively boring slice-of-life essay, and Kunikida produced study columns filled with trivia. Between that and the rest of the material Haruhi'd been dashing around the school to collect (including things like the four-panel comic that someone in the manga club drew for us), the final product was almost too thick for a literature club newsletter. It took quite a bit of effort to staple each individual issue together, and the two hundred issues we printed flew away without us having to run around at all. I guessed that all the running around Haruhi had done had worked as accidental advertising for the project.

As for Haruhi, she wrote material too, just as she'd promised. In addition to a haughty "Letter from the Editor," she wrote a short essay.

"Save the World by Overloading it with Fun, I: A Memo on the Path to the Future" was the title, and her thesis was filled with charts and symbols that, according to Haruhi, were the result of her thoughts on how to ensure the brigade continued indefinitely into the future. As for me, I found it totally incomprehensible. But there was still an order to the chaos, I felt, like Haruhi's mind had somehow overflowed directly onto the page.

But when Asahina read it, she was so stunned she looked as though she might fall over.

"That's...I can't...so this is how..."

Her shock was so total that I was afraid her pupils were going to fall right out of her widely opened eyes, but when I asked her why she was so surprised—

"I can't tell you; the details are classified."

—she said.

"These are the fundamentals of time-plane theory. In my time... um...this is the first thing people like me learn. But who originated it, and when, has always been a mystery...and now, to find out that it was Suzumiya all along..."

She was then rendered speechless. I, likewise, was speechless, as the following notion appeared in my mind:

Haruhi would surely keep at least one copy of the newsletter to bring home with her. It was entirely possible that the bespectacled little boy would have a chance to see it. Haruhi was his tutor, after all. While Asahina and I had ensured a variety of conditions for the boy's future, there were surely more to come. Was Haruhi the ultimate trigger? Even if she wasn't, there seemed to be many composite elements in play. The number of questions I had for Asahina the Elder increased by one.

Having fully distributed the newsletter the same day it was completed, Haruhi made a point of going to the student council room to inform them. That she was practically radiating pride from her body goes without saying.

The president didn't so much as twitch an eyebrow at Haruhi's victorious entry. His glasses shone as he spoke. "A promise is a promise. We'll approve the continued existence of the literature club. However, concerning this 'SOS Brigade' of yours, it is none of our concern. Do not forget that there is quite some time left in my term," he said in a transparent ploy to get one last parting shot in, before turning his back on us.

Haruhi took it as an admission of defeat, and she returned to the clubroom in high spirits, dancing a victory dance with Asahina as Nagato looked on indifferently. So it goes.

In any case, that was the end of that particular madness. All that was left was to wait for spring.

At this rate, so long as nothing happened, we would each of us move on to the next grade. If I had to guess at the next likely point where Haruhi would get up to something, it would be spring break.

Strangely, the year had felt both long and short. It's a secret, but I'm putting a circle on a day in April this year. It's the same day as last year's school entrance ceremony.

Even if everybody forgot, even if Haruhi herself forgot, it's the anniversary of a day I'll always remember.

I'm confident that so long as I live, I'll never forget the day I met Haruhi.

So long as I don't lose my memory, that is.

# WANDERING SHADOW

The smart sound of the ball hitting the gym floor echoed along with shrill cries, bouncing off the ceiling and washing over me.

I was dressed in slightly dirty gym clothes, my hands folded lazily behind my head and my feet stretched out in front of me. I was totally relaxed, and if you wanted to know what I was doing in that totally relaxed state, the simple answer was that I was spectating. After all, I had nothing else to do that day, but simply having nothing to do does not get you out of school; thus I found myself looking down at the scene unfolding below me.

I was sitting on the catwalk that runs along both sides of the gymnasium, a narrow walkway with handrails. I imagine just about every gym has them. I'm not exactly sure what they're for, but at the time there was no doubt that they'd been provided for people like me to observe the competitions below. And I wasn't the only one lazing around up there either.

Taniguchi was doing the same thing, right next to me.

"Damn, our girls are pretty good," he offered, not sounding particularly impressed, despite his words.

"Yeah," I replied vaguely, following the white volleyball as it moved around the court. The ball, falling parabolically down after being grandly served by the opposition, got tossed vertically up in a perfect set.

As I watched the ball come down, a gym clothes–clad girl came running up from well behind the attack line, jumped, and brought her raised hand down with amazing force, converting potential energy into kinetic energy, which was transferred onto the poor ball, which in turn split two opposing blocks and landed in the corner of their court. It was a perfect counterattack, and the volleyball club member who was acting as an umpire blew her whistle.

More cheers echoed through the gym.

Taniguchi must have been really bored. "Hey, Kyon, want to bet on which side's going to win?" he asked unenthusiastically.

It was a good idea, but without a handicap, it might not be a blowout, but it wasn't going to be an even match either.

Before Taniguchi could open his mouth again, I replied, "Class Five's gonna win. No doubt about it."

Taniguchi clucked his tongue. I gave him a sidelong look and continued.

"After all, *she's* on the team."

The girl landed beautifully, right next to the net, and turned around, revealing a daring smile. She wasn't looking up at me, and it was a different smile than the self-satisfied one she used in the clubroom. To the teammates who gathered around her excitedly, it wordlessly said, "This is just too easy!"

It was a one-set match to 15 points.

Just as I predicted, our class—Class 5, year 1—won by double the opponent's score. The ace attacker who was the source of most of their points mingled among her teammates, who were busily high-fiving one another. She, meanwhile, raised her fist and lightly punched the open palms of her team.

As she exited the court's sidelines, she finally noticed us crammed in the catwalk. She stopped and looked up for just a moment, and then I was released from her usual dagger-like gaze.

No matter what she did, she excelled at it, and if it were a contest of any sort, she hated to lose—even going so far as to score nearly all the points in this volleyball game. She—ah, there's no point in being mysterious anymore, obviously it's Haruhi Suzumiya—took a sports drink passed to her by a classmate-turned-teammate and drank it dry.

As I'm sure you've already guessed, there was a tournament on.

It was early March, and with final exams having ended, a school would enter preparations for its next break, and our particular public high school was no exception. As far as the school schedule went, we'd just be waiting for the term to end, but at some point, somebody had gotten the brilliant idea to find something else to do with that time, and as a result, around this time every year the school would hold an intramural sports tournament.

I'm sure the idea was to let us unwind after we'd curdled our brains with exam studying, but if this was their idea of unwinding, I'd rather they just extend the vacation.

Incidentally, soccer was on the boys' menu, while girls would be playing volleyball. I was on Class 1-5's B team, which had lost to our old enemies, Class 1-9, in the first round of the tournament. I didn't consider them enemies just because Koizumi was in that class—it was because 1-9 was on the special math and science course, and as a matter of course was filled with brainiac types, and if we couldn't at least beat them at soccer, we'd be humiliated in front of the other classes. And having lost, we were indeed thus humiliated.

So it was that we'd had nothing better to do than to head over to the gym to watch the girls in their gym uniforms.

"Still, Suzumiya is really amazing," said Kunikida calmly from

a few feet away. The girls' volleyball team had gotten through to the third round, thanks to Haruhi's significant efforts, and we'd been watching since the middle of the second. "Why doesn't she join one of the sports clubs? Talent like hers isn't exactly common."

I agreed wholeheartedly. If Haruhi would just join the track-and-field club, she'd probably be able to qualify for nationals in short-, medium-, and long-distance running. And the same was true for any other sport. She absolutely hated to lose, after all. I never met anyone else so obsessed with being the winner, or being the best.

I looked over to the other court, where there was still a match in progress. "I'm sure she'd tell you she's got more important things to do than waste her youth on sports." I was hoping that maybe Asahina or Nagato would be playing, but I didn't see either of them anywhere in the gym.

"Like the SOS Brigade, eh?" said Taniguchi, chuckling. "Heh, that's just like her. Hard to imagine her doing anything like a normal student. She's been that way since middle school. These days her favorite thing to do is get up to incomprehensible games with you, Kyon."

I wasn't in the mood to refute him.

There wasn't much time left in the school year. The school day had been shortened for the tournament, which automatically lessened the amount of time spent in the classroom. We'd move into the spring break, and just about when the cherry blossoms started to bloom, we'd become second-year students. Then there'd be the reshuffling of classes that worried many a student, which would decide what joys and sorrows the following year would contain. I'd grown fond of these two jerks, and it would've been nice to have them in my classroom the next year, if nothing else.

As I zoned out, Kunikida sat up, which grabbed my attention.

"Looks like the next match is starting."

I looked and saw the girls of Class 1-5 scattering onto the court, with Haruhi, their captain, at the center.

I was ready for spring to arrive at any time, but given the school's position between mountains, the air was still pretty cold. There was an emotional factor that probably added to the feeling of cold—that being the fact that I'd gotten my test results back a few days previous.

The scores weren't too bad, at least by my standards, but they weren't enough to satisfy my mom's hopes, and she'd sent away for pamphlets from cram schools and tutoring centers, leaving them where I'd find them—it was so bad that my stomach hurt. She just wanted me to get into a public university somewhere, and on paper that was my ambition too. Aim high and all that. And plus...how do I put it? There was Haruhi to consider.

The reason my final-exam marks weren't doing their best impression of low-altitude flying was because Haruhi had become a temporary in-house tutor, helping me do last-minute cramming in the clubroom. A few days before the exams started, she'd scattered textbooks and notes all over the table and said this:

"I won't let you take makeup exams or extra lessons. I will not allow you to make mistakes that come between you and your SOS Brigade duties!"

When it came to "SOS Brigade duties," I didn't complain. Before I could even ask what the hourly wage for brigade duties was, my wallet was already empty—not that it mattered.

In any case, even I had to admit that sitting across from Koizumi and drinking Asahina's tea in the clubroom beat getting stared at by a teacher while trying to solve new questions or listening to boring lectures, so I did not resist when Haruhi donned an armband that said "Professor" and delivered her teachings.

Professor Haruhi's method of test taking was extremely simple— she relied on pure speculation to guess which questions would be on the test and studied those heavily. I knew her intuition to be keen indeed, so I was only too happy to go along with her. If I'd asked Nagato, she probably could've just recited every question and an example answer to go along with it, whereas Koizumi could've employed some intrigue to steal the tests out of the staff room, but I resorted to neither supernatural powers nor covert operations and decided to simply apply myself. To be honest, watching Haruhi the house tutor happily brandish her pointer, even going so far as to wear fake glasses, I had no particular desire to use any other method, since it wouldn't actually be in my best interests.

There was no question that Haruhi wanted to sit behind me in class again next year. There was no question that she'd occasionally poke me in the back with her mechanical pencil, regardless of whether class was happening or not, saying, "Hey, Kyon, I've been thinking—" before excitedly launching into an explanation of whatever it was I'd come to wish she hadn't been thinking about. And to do that, she'd have to be in the same class as me, which meant we'd have to be aiming for roughly the same level of college, which naturally led to her having an interest in my grades. I mean, I *was* the SOS Brigade's exclusive errand boy. It was the same way an army made up of only officers would be useless. It was Haruhi's job to give orders, and it was my job to carry things around.

That had been the way things were last year, and I had no doubt that they would continue into next year. That was certainly what Haruhi wanted, and she'd do anything to make her desires reality. We could even wind up repeating this last year over and over into infinity.

Of course, I didn't think anything like the August incident would happen again. Haruhi wouldn't reset the year. I was fairly sure of that.

Why was I so sure? Because I knew that the year that followed the creation of the SOS Brigade had been a lot of fun for Haruhi. Haruhi would never unmake those memories. I was positive.

I could look at the way she was right now and know.

I once again looked at the scene below me.

Haruhi was leading her volleyball team to victory.

She attacked ruthlessly, over and over. I had no interest in the way her shirt fluttered up to reveal her belly button when she jumped. What had my attention was her expression.

Last March, when I'd first met her, Haruhi was completely isolated from the rest of the class. Or should I say, she'd made no effort to fit in, to find a place for herself. Sitting in that chair behind me, she never smiled and was totally closed off, as though she'd taken it upon herself to singlehandedly dampen the mood of the class. Even after that, once she'd started talking to me at least, she was still estranged from the other girls—but not anymore. While she didn't have a particular group she was good friends with, her days of always pushing everyone away were behind her.

It seemed like the creation of the SOS Brigade had pushed her in a good direction. At the same time, she'd always had that ability within herself. It had been during middle school that Haruhi had started having difficulties. I bet that before that she'd had the force of a radar-guided missile and shone with the brilliance of a fiery afterburner—so rather than her having "gotten better," it was more accurate to say that she'd gotten her old self back.

I hadn't known her before the first year of middle school. And even then, I'd only barely glanced at her. I seem to remember wanting to ask someone who'd gone to the same elementary school as her what she'd been like, but I don't think I wound up doing it.

There on the volleyball court, Haruhi and her classmates were enjoying the tournament. But she seemed to be holding back a little. Apparently her full-on hundred-watt brigade chief power was reserved for when she was dreaming up punishment games. Which was too bad. It was a waste not to let it shine here too.

Haruhi nailed another spike, then looked almost embarrassed as she punched her teammates' extended fists.

The tournament came to an end, thus concluding the day's school activities.

Anyone with clubs to attend scattered to do so, while people not in clubs went home. Since the members of the SOS Brigade were assembling in the literature club room, I made my way toward my familiar folding chair with Haruhi, who strode up the stairs in high spirits.

It was obvious that her good mood was due to her victory in the volleyball tournament. It wasn't as though they gained anything by coming out on top, but as I looked at Haruhi walking beside me, I could tell she was extremely pleased. She'd also triumphed against the student council president's attempt to close down the literature club, and I couldn't think of anything else that could drive her to melancholy—except, I suppose, the impending advancement to our second year of high school.

According to Koizumi, more or less anything Haruhi wished for would come to pass, so it wouldn't surprise me if Nagato, Koizumi, and I wound up all in the same class along with Haruhi. Koizumi was in a special class, but I was sure Haruhi's Haruhi-brand power could do something about that. Compared to making energy beams shoot out of Asahina's eyes, it would be trivial. The problem was that Haruhi didn't know she had such power, so it was also possible we'd wind up scattered among classes.

She still didn't know—neither about Nagato's data-manipulation ability, nor about the kinds of things Koizumi's Agency could accomplish.

So I was optimistic. I'll be completely honest—next year, I hoped I got to sit in front of Haruhi again. If we got scattered, I'd probably feel the way I felt just before Christmas, when I'd discovered her disappearance. I'd be constantly wondering what she was getting up to.

On the other hand, I wondered if that might not be such a bad thing after all. Was that a self-contradiction? But again, just as Koizumi said, if that meant Haruhi's powers were calming down, that would be good.

But wait—the truth is, I *would* feel a bit lonely.

"What's your problem?" I must've been making a pretty introspective face. Haruhi peered down at me from the top of the stairs. "You're acting weird. First you were smiling, and now you're all serious. Do you have some kind of facial disorder? Or are you still dwelling on getting your butt kicked at soccer? Honestly, the boys of Class Five are totally useless."

That was because the field positions for the tournament had been decided by lottery, I said. All the athletic guys wound up on team A. The defender line was Taniguchi, Kunikida, and me. I'll admit it was pretty nice to be able to tackle the hell out of the Class 9 forwards, but unfortunately I couldn't keep up with their captain, Koizumi, who kept kicking these killer passes. But even Class 9 lost to Class 6 in the next round, which was an appropriately half-assed result for Koizumi. I almost wondered if he did it on purpose, and I said as much.

"What're you talking about?" Haruhi laughed. "But yeah, I can see Koizumi doing something like that. I mean, it *is* Class Nine. When guys like you and Taniguchi decide you hate the smart kids and decide to charge them, you're gonna get hurt and look stupid. I'll admit there are a few jerks in the class, but I like most of the Class Nine students just fine."

She'd liked them well enough to transport all of them to a different school with her. Oh, wait, no—that had been Nagato's doing.

As I was untangling the threads of my memory, we arrived at the clubroom. Haruhi seemed to have forgotten to make even the slightest gesture toward politeness, and she slammed the door open without so much as knocking. "Hey, Mikuru! How'd the tournament go? And is there any cold tea? I got really thirsty playing all that volleyball. I bet I'm dehydrated."

She strode right into the room and flopped into the brigade chief's seat.

The rest of the brigade members had already assembled, and I was greeted by the familiar sight of Nagato and Koizumi in their usual places, with Asahina in that maid outfit that suited her so well—she could've been the subject of a Rembrandt or a Rubens.

"I don't have anything cold, I'm sorry," said Asahina, apologizing for the mistake. "Ah, shall I chill it for you? In the refrigerator?"

That's right, this room had a fridge. It was a tiny one without a freezer box, but we'd used it to cool soft drinks back when we'd made stew. Since my main drink in here was Asahina's hot tea, I had even less use for the refrigerator than I did for the portable gas burner.

"Nah, it's okay," said Haruhi generously. "That'd take too much time, and tea's better when it's just been brewed anyway."

Cups of tea were quickly brought to Haruhi and me. Asahina's facility with tea had leveled up again. Just as I was debating whether to compliment her on the improvement in one of her hospitality skills, Asahina spoke very happily.

"Cold tea...hmm, yes, I suppose I could get a refrigerator with a water cooler next time."

What was she talking about? Sometimes I wondered whether she'd brought back knowledge from the future on any subject other than tea making, although I would never say so out loud. I didn't want her flailing around too much. While she looked like nothing other than an adorable maid, a time traveler was a time traveler, and if Asahina got too hasty, she could easily start going on about the nature of time, and unlike Koizumi, I got a headache when I tried to think about that stuff. I wanted a break from incomprehensible diagrams.

Speaking of Koizumi, he was sitting in his own chair, playing single-player Othello.

"Now that really takes me back," I said, looking at Koizumi's activity. Come to think of it, this was the first board game that had been brought into the clubroom. And I'd brought it.

"Indeed. It'll soon be a year since we all met. I was thinking it would be nice to bring things back around to the beginning."

He'd been fairly agreeable during the soccer match, but sitting here in the clubroom, Koizumi seemed even happier, and before I could reply, he'd reset the Othello board to its original state.

Back to the beginning, eh?

I hadn't lived so long I could really look back on the past, but they were words I could see myself saying.

As I picked up one of the magnetized Othello pieces, I looked sideways. Othello. One year ago. Those words had a very particular association in my mind, and the object of that association was sitting at a corner of the table, quietly absorbed in a book on foreign literature.

" . . . "

Yuki Nagato silently read her book. The first time I saw this alien-humanoid interface show something like a genuine emotion was when Asahina and I were playing Othello in this very room. The memory is very clear.

When I thought about it, I realized I hadn't seriously played a game like this with Nagato. Unless she lost on purpose, I couldn't

imagine I'd have a chance at winning. Unlike playing against Koizumi, when I usually won. Unless that was on purpose too. Could be.

Be all that as it may, Haruhi sat at her brigade chief's desk and was quiet for a time. At first she used the computer—doing some web surfing was part of her routine. Of course, the first thing she did upon opening the browser was to load up the SOS Brigade's crappy site, thereby increasing the hit counter by one. She considered this one of her duties. She'd then browse through paranormal activity sites, occasionally installing random pieces of freeware she found, such that I had no idea what was or was not on the computer anymore. Occasionally she'd run into a problem, and it was inevitably the computer club president who'd be called in to help. I guess it was nice to have the right man for the job.

The lovely, pre-spring afternoon, with everybody assembled and relaxing, just a little bit tired from the sports tournament—it felt pretty nice.

My Othello game was going well, and Asahina's tea was delicious. I would be able to pass the rest of the day uneventfully and go home without incident.

—Or at least, that would've been nice, but such peaceful days do not last forever.

Back to the beginning.

Yes, that was what I found myself wanting to mutter when the client came right into the SOS Brigade.

That's right, a client. It wasn't somebody we'd arranged to have come, nor was it the result of one of Haruhi's unplanned fancies.

After knocking, the client timidly entered the room, like a tiny deer invited to a bear's den, then said something calculated to delight Haruhi.

There was a place near her house where ghosts were rumored to emerge, she said. She wanted to know if we could look into it.

\*     \*     \*

"Ghosts?!" Haruhi parroted, her eyes shining. "Emerging, you say?"

"Yes," said Sakanaka, nodding seriously. "It's a rumor in my neighborhood. That there are ghosts."

Sakanaka...I couldn't remember her first name, but she was a classmate of Haruhi's and mine in Class 5. Sakanaka sat down on the folding chair we used for guests, accepting some tea from Asahina, her face clouded as she explained.

"It's only recently that the story started. Maybe three days ago. I'd been thinking something weird was happening..."

She tilted the guest-use-only teacup to her lips, looking bemusedly around the room—particularly at the clothing rack containing all of Asahina's costumes.

I thought back to Haruhi's volleyball matches. On the girls' A team there had been a particular setter who'd supported Haruhi the attacker very well—it was this girl, Sakanaka.

To be perfectly honest, she'd never made much of an impression on me in class. Or rather, the most impression-leaving person in Class 5 had been Asakura, but she's gone now, and nobody had really risen up to take her place. I wasn't even sure who our class rep was. When I thought about it that way, Taniguchi and Kunikida were closer to Haruhi than the rest of our class was. To put it in terms of distance from Earth, they were Mars, but she was Uranus.

However, Haruhi didn't care about details like intra-class distance one bit.

"I'd just love to hear the details. Ghosts...yes, ghosts. Sakanaka, are you absolutely sure there are ghosts? If so, it is no overstatement to say that the SOS Brigade must unquestionably spring into action!"

She looked ready to slap on an armband that said, "Paranormal Investigator," head to the scene, and start stringing up black-and-yellow Do Not Enter tape.

"Wait. Please, Suzumiya—wait!" said Sakanaka hastily, waving her hands. "I'm not positive there are ghosts. It just seems... ghost-ish, I guess? Something like that. It's only a rumor. But I do think that spot is strange..."

Sakanaka was now the focus of everyone else in the room, including Nagato. Suddenly realizing our collective gaze was on her, she shrank back.

"Um...maybe I shouldn't have said anything...?"

"No, you totally should have, Sakanaka!" shouted Haruhi. "Whether they be demons or vengeful spirits, suicides or playful ghosts, I don't care! If it means I can meet a ghost, I'll buy a ticket anywhere. Anyway, I can't hear a story like that and then just sit around doing nothing."

Of course, she pretty much *never* sat around doing nothing, I pointed out.

"Kyon, I'll ask you to keep your smart-aleck mouth shut for once. We're talking about *ghosts* here! Don't you want to see one? Have you *ever* seen one?"

I had not. And I wanted to continue that forever, I said.

With the energy of a kindergartener who'd woken up from her afternoon nap only half an hour earlier, Haruhi said, "But if one happened to appear in front of me, I'd really want to talk to it a little!"

Sorry. I wouldn't.

I looked away from Haruhi's burning gaze, turning my eyes to Sakanaka, who seemed like she wanted to say something, then kept suddenly closing her mouth.

Why had Sakanaka brought this ghost case to us all of a sudden, right here at the very end of the school year? She was only our second client. After Kimidori...after Kimidori had come to us for the consultation session that led to the cave-cricket incident, I'd torn down our "clients wanted" poster and thrown it in the garbage, which seemed to have worked, since we hadn't had another student coming and mistaking us for a general-purpose troubleshooting agency. Had Sakanaka seen the poster while it was up on the bulletin board and remembered it all this time? If so, she should probably have been using that excellent memory to remember something a little more worthwhile.

I said as much, and much to my surprise, Sakanaka shook her head.

"No, that's not it. I remembered something else. Someone had handed it to me, and I hadn't thrown it away; I just put it in a drawer in my house. That was what reminded me…"

Sakanaka produced a single piece of paper from her book bag. It was old and crumpled, and when Asahina saw what it was, she backed away from it like a vampire from a cross.

"Th-that's…"

It was the source of Asahina's trauma and the fruit of the SOS Brigade's very first activity, despite being a simple flyer produced by wasting school copier resources.

It contained the SOS Brigade's declaration of founding.

This was what I was sure was written on the flyer:

"We, the SOS Brigade, are searching for the world's mysteries. People who've experienced mysterious phenomena in the past, are currently experiencing mysterious phenomena, or plan to experience mysterious phenomena in the future should come to us for a consultation. We will help you find resolution. It's true."

Two bunny girls had stood at the school gate to pass out that flyer as part of Haruhi's effort to seize the world's mysteries.

This was ridiculous. To think the seed she planted with that flyer would eventually bear fruit.

And just when the school year was about to end without incident too. Who had wished for this curtain call? We didn't have an encore prepared. This was no time to be going back to the beginning.

As though she'd picked up on Asahina's and my feelings,

Sakanaka sounded uneasy. "...This *is* the SOS Brigade, right? It's pretty famous now...That's what you and your friends do, right, Suzumiya? Like in horror movies and stuff."

Sorry, Sakanaka. We didn't have anybody who specialized in horror. All we had was an alien bookworm, a mystery-loving esper, and a time traveler who was pretty easy on the eyes. If we had a genre, it was probably sci-fi. And even that much would be beyond me.

I'd fallen into silence. Haruhi spoke up against me, more and more excited. "See, Kyon! People *are* paying attention. It wasn't a waste at all. I *knew* those flyers were a good idea."

I wondered about that. I had a suspicion that Haruhi herself had forgotten she'd made them until now.

"Cheer up, Sakanaka! You're a classmate, so we'll take on this case for free."

To be completely truthful, no matter who came to us with a case, Haruhi would never ask for money. For her, the greatest reward was the fact of having a mystery to solve at all. She was satisfied as soon as the client walked in the door. I knew that perfectly well thanks to the cave-cricket incident last year.

"Ghosts, huh?" Haruhi smiled lazily. "The last thing we'll do is banish them, but before we do that we'll need to hear everything about them. We're gonna need a camera for documentation and a video camera for interviews."

She was getting really into it, totally ignoring me and the other brigade members. This was bad. At this rate, ghosts might actually start appearing. Except what about Sakanaka's story?

Ghost sightings were the result of people's easily confused sense of vision being mistaken, or hearing something that was just actually dry grass under a willow tree rustling. If a real ghost actually showed up, it'd mean the upending of all of humanity's accumulated scientific knowledge.

Even Sakanaka wasn't sure. "Please, just wait a minute," she said. "I don't know for sure that it's a ghost. I might be wrong. I just can't think of anything else…" Her resolve was starting to sound half-baked.

"Hey, Haruhi," I interrupted hastily, since Haruhi had already started hurrying toward the equipment closet. "Calm down, okay? Let's listen to what Sakanaka has to say. The situation isn't that simple."

"Don't get in my way," grumbled Haruhi, but she returned to her desk and folded her arms. Neither Sakanaka nor I could hide our relief. Now I finally had time to check Nagato's and Koizumi's expressions.

I probably shouldn't have looked.

Neither of them looked any different from normal. In other words, Koizumi had his usual meaningless smile, and Nagato's expression was totally blank. Like always.

However, both of them were watching Sakanaka, apparently keenly interested in her. For some reason I got the sense that matching words were written on both their faces.

—*Ghosts? What is this person talking about?*

Or something along those lines.

Now then, while I'm giving my views on things, I should say that I don't believe in ghosts. I'm firmly convinced that those "paranormal documentaries" you see on TV are nothing more than well-crafted entertainment.

Of course, this conviction is like a house built in the sand, given that I'd found myself stuck in a group with an alien, a time traveler, and an esper, and spent a lot of time getting involved in all sorts of supernatural nonsense.

So somewhere in my mind I felt it was entirely possible that a ghost, phantom, or wraith might decide to pop out of somewhere if it got the notion to do so. But just as I've never met a person from another dimension, I've never so much as said hello to a ghost, and since there's no point in worrying about a being you've never met, I sprinted away from such concerns. If they were going to come, then let them come! But I wasn't going to go looking for them. Does my lot in life make any more sense now?

But really, all I could do was act aloof. And as for the other members—

"Ghosts, you say? How interesting." Koizumi put a finger to his chin, apparently deep in thought.

"Um...is that, er...?" Asahina looked imploringly at the client with questioning eyes.

Nagato, as usual:

"..."

It seemed that, save Haruhi, the entire brigade felt the same way I did—neither Nagato, Koizumi, nor Asahina really had much of a serious expression on their faces upon hearing the word "ghost." Asahina in particular looked as if she barely had any conception of what the term meant. Perhaps traditions like religion and ancestor worship don't exist in the future. I'd have to ask about that later. Not that she would tell me.

I might not have been the most outgoing person in the world, but it wasn't like the only people in Class 5 I talked to were Haruhi, Taniguchi, and Kunikida; I exchanged small talk with plenty of my other classmates, although admittedly the range of communication I used was somewhat more constricted when that classmate was a girl.

Groping around the inside of my brain, I could find no memories of having talked to Sakanaka, so it was hard to be sure, but I had the feeling that she wasn't exactly a conversationalist.

So I'll just relate the highlights of the conversation.

"Um, the first time I noticed something was strange was with Rousseau," said Sakanaka, facing Haruhi.

"Rousseau?" said Haruhi, brows knitting.

"Yes. Rousseau is my family's dog."

That dog sure had a hell of a name.

"I take him for a walk every morning and evening. When I first got him, I used to take him on all sorts of different routes, but now I do the same walk every time. I've just totally gotten used to it—"

That wasn't really important, I pointed out.

"Sorry. But it might be important."

Which part, I wanted to know.

"Shut up, Kyon," said Haruhi. "Sakanaka, please continue."

"I was on the same route as always, and Rousseau was happily walking along, but th-then..." She stumbled over her words, speaking quietly. Was she performing a ghost story now?

"About a week ago, Rousseau started hating that path. He'd pull on the leash, like this—"

Sakanaka made a pose like an animal clinging to the ground. It looked just like Shamisen did when he didn't want to move from a warm spot.

"He'd get like this, and he wouldn't budge. He'd be fine halfway but then suddenly stop. It seemed so strange. And it was always like that. So I changed the route I used."

Having gotten that far in her story, Sakanaka sipped some tea.

So her dog with the philosopher's name had suddenly started hating the route by which he was walked. So where did ghosts enter the story?

My question was Haruhi's question, evidently.

"What about the ghosts?"

"Like I said." Sakanaka set down her teacup. "I don't know if there *are* ghosts. It's just a rumor."

I told her we'd like to hear the source of the rumor.

"There are many. Lots of people have dogs in my neighborhood. I often chat with them when I'm out walking Rousseau, and he's happy to see his friends, so I've gotten to know a lot of people in the area. The first was Mrs. Anan with her two shelties. She said the same thing, that when she walks them, she doesn't even try to go down that street. Because her dogs started refusing to go."

But humans could walk by without feeling anything? I asked.

"That's right. I didn't feel anything weird."

We were getting off topic, I said. What was important was the notion of ghosts.

"Right, yes." Sakanaka's face clouded. "Since that day, none of the neighborhood dogs will approach that area. All the owners are talking about it. There used to be some stray cats there too, but they've all disappeared..."

Haruhi was listening carefully. She had a pen and paper as though to take notes, but when I sneaked a look, all she'd drawn were some scrawled dogs and cats. Then, she seemed to seize upon the rough logical progression.

"So what you're saying is that there's a ghost in the area, which is why animals won't go near it? That only cats and dogs can see it, and it's invisible to humans?"

"Yes. That's the story that's going around." Sakanaka nodded firmly. "There's another thing that bothers me. There's a girl named Higuchi, and she has a bunch of dogs. Her puppies are friends with my dog." She sounded terrified as she continued. "But one of them has gotten sick recently. He wasn't out for a walk this morning. I didn't have time to hear the details, but apparently he's been taken to an animal hospital." Sakanaka implored Haruhi with serious eyes. "Don't you think that sounds like a ghost, Suzumiya?"

"Hmm, well..." Haruhi rested her chin on her folded arms, narrowing her eyes as she thought about it. She seemed to be thinking that there wasn't much to this story, and that it would be a lot more interesting if there were ghosts involved. "At the present, I can't be sure."

It was a surprisingly prudent answer coming from Haruhi, but then the corner of her mouth quirked.

"But there's a large possibility it is! They do say that dogs and cats can see things humans can't. And maybe Mr. Whatever's dog saw a ghost and got sick, then passed out from the shock."

I couldn't exactly raise my hand and shout, "Objection!" to this. After all, I saw Shamisen staring intently at a corner of the room with nothing in it all the time. I'm pretty sure most cat owners would agree with me, but who knows. But unlike dogs, even if a cat did see a ghost, it wouldn't fall ill from the shock. The cat owners out there know what I'm talking about.

As I was summoning the memory of the calico cat at my house, Haruhi jumped out of her chair. "I've got the gist of things."

The only "gist" I had was that there was an area that cats and dogs refused to enter, I said.

"That's more than enough. There's nothing more to be gained in hypothesizing. We should head immediately to the scene. There must be something there that's making animals sense danger—like a ghost, ghoul, or demon."

Or something even worse. Imagining the formless monsters that roamed communistically around nineteenth century Europe gave me a chill. Depending on how we communicated with it, we might be able to lead a ghost to enlightenment, whereas with a ghoul or a demon we might need to find a Ghostbuster or a demon postbox. But what if some unnameable cosmic horror emerged to possess us—what then?

I naturally looked toward Nagato when the thought occurred to me.

Our last client had been Kimidori, the student council secretary, and she'd been connected to Nagato. Perhaps Sakanaka was too...

But I quickly abandoned this notion, because Nagato was looking up from her book, her interest surprisingly drawn by

Sakanaka's story. On her pale white face was an expression only I could read—I was quite proud of myself for this. Her expression was shifted one micron toward looking contemplative. Which meant that the story Sakanaka was sharing with us was an irregularity, from Nagato's perspective.

I took the opportunity to check Koizumi's expression. When I caught his eye, he shrugged minutely and smirked. Annoyingly, he seemed to have discerned exactly what I wanted to say. *This isn't my doing*, his posture conveyed, and I hated myself for knowing Koizumi well enough to read his body language so well.

As for the third party's state, it went without saying. Everything about Asahina broadcasted the fact that she had nothing to do with this—she could barely keep up with the conversation. Even if the source of the ghost-whatever had something to do with time travel, Asahina wasn't involved—excluding Asahina the Elder, of course.

"All right, everyone," Haruhi said spiritedly. "We're heading out! Bring the camera, and...well, I guess we don't have any ghost-capturing equipment. I wish we had some paper talismans with Tangut writing on them."

"What we need is a city map," added Koizumi, aiming his smile at Sakanaka. "I'd like to do some interviewing. Can I ask for the cooperation of your dog, Rousseau?"

It looked like Koizumi was on board. We hadn't found any mysterious phenomena during our citywide patrols, but now we had a specific spot that we could jump straight into.

"Sure." Sakanaka nodded at Koizumi's handsome face. "If it's during one of Rousseau's walks."

Asahina blinked her eyes in surprise. "Oh, um, I had better get changed." She hastily smoothed her maid outfit. Asahina seemed to be worried that if she didn't hurry and change, she'd get dragged out wearing what she had on, and Haruhi was certainly capable of doing so.

"Good point, Mikuru. You do need to change. That outfit's not suited to this at all," said Haruhi reasonably.

"N-no, it's not," said Asahina, sounding relieved as she reached up to take the kerchief off her head.

Which meant that it was time for Koizumi and me to make ourselves scarce. Whether or not I got to, I definitely wasn't going to let Koizumi get a free peek.

I was turning to leave the room when Haruhi said something unexpected.

"But you're not going to change into your school uniform."

"Wha?" Asahina made a noise of confusion as I walked past her, as Haruhi strode over to the hanger rack. She cheerily selected an outfit and pulled it out. "Here, this one! This is perfect for dealing with ghosts, right?"

The outfit that Haruhi had produced involved a white robe and scarlet hakama trousers. It was one of the classic costumes of old Japan.

Asahina couldn't help backing away.

"Um…that is…"

"It's a shrine maiden!" Haruhi smiled the special smile she reserved for when she'd had a really great idea, pushing the outfit against Asahina. "This is perfect for exorcisms! I don't have any priest robes, and even if I did I'd have to shave your head to make you look right in 'em, and I'd feel kinda bad about that. What do you think, Kyon? I don't pick costumes without thinking about it! Look, this is gonna come in handy!"

I wondered whether a maid or a shrine maiden would draw more attention leaving the school, but before I could voice my reaction, Koizumi and I were shooed out of the clubroom door and into the hallway.

From inside the room, I heard the familiar sound of Haruhi's delight at making Asahina change, mingled with Asahina's adorable cries of dismay at the same.

I figured I might as well take the opportunity to ask.

"Koizumi."

"Yes? I'll just say up front that there's nothing obvious that comes to mind when I hear the word 'ghost.'" Koizumi brushed his hair aside with a finger, smiling placidly.

"So what the hell is it?"

"I can't say anything for certain at the moment. It would be pure conjecture."

Conjecture's fine, I told him. Just give it to me.

"The situation is that all the neighborhood dogs have started avoiding a certain location. So here's a quiz for you: what is it that animals, and dogs in particular, are much better at than humans?"

"Sense of smell."

"Exactly. There is a possibility that somewhere along the course where Sakanaka used to walk her dog, something that gives off a scent that dogs hate is buried." Koizumi pushed a wisp of hair behind his ear and continued, his smile never wavering. "One possibility is that there's some kind of chemical weapon in the area. It might have fallen there while being transported by a paramilitary organization."

That was ridiculous. They wouldn't carry chemical weapons on the back of a little truck where it could easily fall off, I pointed out.

"Another possibility would be radiation. Of course, I'm not sure how sensitive animals are to atomic radiation."

Forget all this talk about chemical weapons. An unexploded bomb seemed more likely to me, I said.

"Indeed, that is also possible. Or if we're speaking more realistically, perhaps a bear came down out of the mountains and is hibernating in the area, and the dogs can sense that it's about to awaken…"

No way. There might be wild boars in the mountains around town, but there weren't any bears, I said.

"Essentially," Koizumi said, folding his arms elegantly, "given the vague information we have now, we can think of any number of possibilities. The one and only way to see through to the truth will be a combination of gathering all the evidence, using logical inference and lateral thinking, and adding a little bit of gut instinct to direct our actions. The most important one of those is having definite information. Have we gotten all the clues available? Being sure of that is no easy task."

If he wanted to give a lecture on mystery-solving methods, he should've been doing it at the mystery club. We weren't going to figure anything out by just thinking about it. With something like this, it was just as Haruhi said—we were going to have to go to the scene and look for anything strange. It'd be obvious once we got there. If she decided to start digging, we might wind up excavating ancient coins from back when Himiko was the first empress of Japan, which would bring archaeologists from miles around—I didn't really want to think about that, but anyway, if he wanted to do another mystery plot, he should wait until our next club trip, I told him.

"Revealing the truth via pure deduction is the epitome of the mystery genre. There's no fun in an incident whose cause is obvious upon quick investigation."

As he was speaking incomprehensibly, Koizumi removed himself from leaning on the door to the clubroom and stepped aside.

At the same time, the door opened, and through it bravely strode our brigade chief, dragging Asahina behind her.

"Preparations complete! You look great, Mikuru! You'll be able to banish any spirit you like with this on!"

"Mmn..."

Out came Shrine Maiden Asahina, timidly looking down as she stepped forth. I hadn't seen this event since the hinamatsuri event on March 3.

I didn't know when it had been made, but wearing that priestess outfit, Asahina was even carrying a ceremonial staff. If she waved it around and chanted the appropriate prayers, unquiet spirits weren't the only things that would be sent to heaven. She was adorable.

Behind them followed Sakanaka, shaking her head as if to say, "You didn't have to go to these lengths," and then Nagato, herself walking like a ghost that happened not to be transparent. Our preparations to depart the school were complete.

I wanted to think that there wouldn't be any actual exorcisms, mostly because of the person on whom we'd foisted the duty. If the part-time shrine maiden cosplayer waved her staff around and actually pulled it off, I'd feel like we'd owe the actual sorcerers and diviners of the Heian period an apology.

Heck, spring was here. This time of year could drive cats and dogs a little crazy. Who's to say humans were any different?

At least, that's what I would've liked to think.

Unfortunately, when Haruhi gets that look of anticipation on her face, the odds of us getting wrapped up in something totally bizarre are very good. On top of that, lately Koizumi, Asahina, and Nagato had been bringing their own incidents to the fore, and it was enough to make me think that maybe I should be causing some trouble of my own.

Of course, such thoughts were folly, as I was the only member of the brigade without ties to some crazy organization.

As I thought about today's events, I considered that the girl who'd brought this case to us seemed like a totally normal, dog-loving girl no matter how I looked at her, and I simply couldn't imagine her dreaming up a prank where she led us to a haunted street, so there was no way an actual ghost would show up. If there really were obvious spirits that Asahina could banish wandering around the city, I got the feeling that they would've made it to the clubroom long ago. And for one thing, this was the wrong season for ghosts, anyway; the Bon Festival wouldn't happen for another few months.

Such were my thoughts as I rested my eyes by gazing at Asahina in her shrine-maiden costume.

Man.

I never thought for one second that something even harder to explain than a ghost would appear in front of us.

To get to Sakanaka's house, we walked down the hill from school to the local train stop, got on the train, switched to a main line, and took it another stop to her neighborhood. It was the opposite direction from the station the SOS Brigade used as its usual meeting point, so I wasn't familiar with the area, but as I recalled, it was a pretty high-class residential district.

Even people who didn't live there knew the place's name was famous for having a lot of celebrities and so on, from what I'd heard, and it proved that Sakanaka was a real high-class girl. Her father was an executive at some construction or architecture firm, and her brother was studying medicine at a big-name university, and it was hard for me to believe I was learning this about a classmate of mine so late in the term.

"It's really not that big of a deal!" said Sakanaka on the train, waving her hands humbly. "The company where my dad works isn't that big, and my big brother's at a public university."

That just said to me he was smart enough not to waste his money. But anyway—

Sakanaka's brother got called "big brother" by his younger sister. It made me feel pleasantly nostalgic, hearing those words.

I thought of my little sister's giggling face and looked around the train.

Since we were all on our way to Sakanaka's home, we were traveling in a group. I got the feeling that our group—the entire SOS Brigade plus one classmate—was just a bit too big for people to think we were just friends heading home, but we still didn't stick out too badly on the train. For one thing, the train was filled with other students commuting home. Students from Koyoen Academy were especially numerous—honestly, the train was packed with 'em—and we North High students were forced into a corner by their private-school girl powers and their curious gazes.

"Umm..."

The reason for the stares was Asahina, who was on the verge of tears as she hung on to a strap in the train car.

To be fair, there was no way a shrine maiden on a crowded train car wasn't gonna get stared at, and when you consider that even a real shrine maiden doesn't commute in the white kimono and crimson trousers, it would've been weirder if she *weren't* getting any attention.

Of course, Asahina had ridden a train and run around a shopping area wearing a bunny-girl costume in the past, and I hoped she found the lack of exposed skin at least some consolation.

Of course, the culprit responsible for forcing Asahina into the shrine-maiden clothing, Haruhi, was totally ignorant of the curious gazes of her fellow train riders.

"Mikuru, spells or chants to use on evil spirits will probably come in handy—do you know any?"

"...N-no, I don't..." Asahina answered quietly, curling in on herself even more.

"I guess I'm not surprised," said Haruhi, who in contrast to the humiliated Asahina was totally cheerful. She turned to Nagato. "Have you read anything about demon-banishing or exorcism in those books of yours?"

"..."

Nagato had been staring out the window at the passing scenery, but she slowly inclined her head. She moved it back, taking about two seconds to do so.

I felt like I understood what she was trying to say, and so did Haruhi.

"Huh. Okay," Haruhi said agreeably. "I guess it's no surprise you don't remember those kinds of details. But don't worry; I know one, so I'll just have you chant that one, okay, Mikuru?"

What was she gonna make Mikuru chant? If it wound up summoning something weird, she'd better be the one to take responsibility for it and not Mikuru, I said.

"That's stupid," said Haruhi delightedly. "If I knew something that awesome, I would've used it a long time ago! No, actually I tried it in middle school. I bought a book of black magic and did just what it said. But nothing happened. In my experience, everything written in books you can get via the usual distribution channels is worthless. Oh, I've got a great idea."

For just a moment, I thought I saw a lightbulb flicker on in the air above Haruhi's head. Apparently she'd thought of another terrible idea.

"Next time we go on a city patrol, we should visit some used bookstores and antique shops. We'll target dingy old shops with suspicious owners and look for real magic books or ceremonial artifacts. Like the kind where a genie appears when you rub it!"

That'd be all well and good if it were the kind that just grants your three wishes, then disappears politely back into its bottle, but knowing Haruhi, we'd release some kind of dark god that would try to plunge the world into terror. Somehow all this talk of banishing evil spirits had turned into the precise opposite of that, and all I could do was quietly hope that all the vintage bookstores and antique shops in the city would close before she discovered them.

Standing next to me, Koizumi chuckled as though he'd read my mind. Since both his hands were full—one with his own book bag and one with Asahina's—he wasn't able to hold on to a strap, and thus swayed with the train's movement. Incidentally I also carried an extra bag over my shoulder; it contained Asahina's school uniform. I wanted her to at least be able to change into it before she went home. If she'd left it in the clubroom, she'd be forced to either come to school tomorrow wearing the shrine-maiden costume or skip school entirely. And if she skipped school, who was going to make tea in the clubroom?

"Do not worry," said Koizumi easily. "While I might not be able to make tea, Asahina's school commute is simple. I can simply send a car to take her to and from," he continued, shutting me up.

I imagined the "car" he mentioned would be something connected with the Agency. If it were just Arakawa, that would be fine, but I got a strange feeling from Mori, whose age I'd never been able to determine. It was enough to make me wonder if she were actually Koizumi's superior. And I'd feel even less comfortable if it were someone besides those two. And while I still owed the Agency for helping out when Asahina'd been kidnapped, I didn't want to owe them any more, I said.

Koizumi chuckled again. "I'll make sure to tell Mori about that. I'm sure it will make her grin."

The train bumped and swayed, and then began to slow. Our station would be coming up soon.

Now was not the time to be worrying about the organizational map of the Agency, nor the agenda of Haruhi's next citywide patrol.

I wondered what we would find on Sakanaka's dog's walking route.

Once we disembarked from the train, we wound up heading back toward the hills, led by Sakanaka. However, unlike the road that led to North High, it was a comparatively less steep city street, and everybody we saw walking on it was somehow fashionable. Fortunately, our group with its shrine maiden did not have to answer any unpleasant questions from an overzealous police officer as we made our way to Sakanaka's house, which took about fifteen minutes.

"Here we are."

Looking at the building to which Sakanaka pointed so easily was enough to make me mutter a few choice words regarding the unfortunate circumstances of my own birth—that's how grand of a house it was. Everything about the three-story building exuded an aura of "a wealthy person lives here," from the outer walls to the entryway to the open, grassy lawn.

While it didn't have the magnitude of sheer area that Tsuruya's purely Japanese-style mansion has, even a common high school student like me could feel its modern grandeur. There was a security company's label next to the family nameplate, and two very nice domestic cars were parked under a roofed garage, with space left over for a third. I wondered how many good deeds I would have to perform to be reborn into a place like this.

As I was standing there feeling sort of discouraged, Sakanaka pushed open the front gate and beckoned Haruhi inside. Haruhi being Haruhi, she strode on in as if she belonged there, with Nagato, Koizumi, and Asahina following. I brought up the rear.

"Wait just a moment." Sakanaka produced a key from her book bag, slotting it into the keyhole of the door to the house's entryway. The door had three separate locks. "It's kind of a pain," said Sakanaka as she unlocked them with practiced ease. I wondered if nobody was home, but no—evidently her mother was in. I guess they just tended to keep the doors locked.

Haruhi looked out over the yard. "Where's the dog?"

"Mmm, he'll be here in a second."

No sooner had Sakanaka opened the door—

"Arf!" cried the white ball of fur that came bounding out the front door. He wagged his short tail like crazy as he jumped up at Sakanaka's skirt.

"Wah…He's so cute…" Asahina squatted down, her eyes shining. The white dog put his paw in her offered hand, then ran circles around the shrine maiden, round eyes gleaming. I had no doubt that there was a certificate somewhere of his purebred lineage.

"Rousseau, sit."

The well-trained dog sat immediately upon hearing his master's command. Asahina rubbed Rousseau's head. "Um, can I hold him?"

"Sure, go ahead."

Asahina clumsily picked up the little dog, and little Rousseau whiffled while licking this new person's face. If I could be reborn as a dog like this in my next life, being a dog wouldn't be so bad.

"This is Rousseau? He's like a little battery-powered toy! What kind of dog is he?" asked Haruhi, petting the head of the well-bred and well-mannered dog that Asahina held.

"He's a West Highland White Terrier, I believe," said Koizumi, beating Sakanaka to the tongue-twisting breed name in a shameless attempt to pander to her.

"You know quite a bit," said Sakanaka, looking down fondly at the little guy Asahina held. "Isn't he cute?"

He *was* pretty cute. With his curly white fur and partially hidden black eyes, he looked like a stuffed animal. In breeding and social caste, he was far removed indeed from the former alley cat that wandered around my house these days. Although Shamisen did have his virtues, as a cat.

Nagato stared intently at the white terrier for around ten seconds, as though she herself were Shamisen, but eventually seemed to lose interest in him and turned her gaze elsewhere. Hmm, it seemed that the number of things in which she was interested was low, and this dog was not among them.

"C'mon, Mikuru, how long are you going to hog him for? I wanna play with him too!"

At Haruhi's words, Asahina reluctantly handed over Rousseau, who seemed to be excited at the prospect of so many new people, and he leaped into Haruhi's arms. Her way of holding him was rather clumsy too, but he seemed not to care, wagging his tail anyway.

"He's so fluffy! Aren't you, Jean-Jacques?"

C'mon, Haruhi, don't go giving other people's dogs nicknames, I wanted to say, but before I could—

"Ha ha! Suzumiya, that's the same nickname my dad uses on him."

Somehow Haruhi had managed to have the same sense of humor as Sakanaka's father, and she unconcernedly lifted the dog-with-a-philosopher's-name above her head. "So, Jean-Jacques here sniffed something out along his walking route, did he? Is that right?"

She was addressing the dog, but of course he didn't answer and instead merely wagged his tail. His owner nodded.

"Yes. Well, but I don't know if it's anything mysterious or not. It's not just Rousseau, though, it's other dogs too, and it freaks me out. Which is where the ghost rumor came from."

It seemed to me that Sakanaka and her various dog-owning acquaintances were jumping to conclusions, but since I knew of the existence of beings just as mysterious as ghosts—aliens, time travelers, and espers, for example—maybe that's just what you'd expect me to think. But Nagato, Asahina, and Koizumi were all physical beings that you could see with your eyes. What was invisible, yet caused dogs to freak out? A genuine unquiet spirit? Surely not.

After that, Sakanaka invited us into her house to have some tea, but Haruhi turned the invitation down, wanting to head to the mysterious place in question as soon as possible, and when Sakanaka went inside to change, she passed by her mother, who'd come out into the entryway. No matter how I looked at her, Sakanaka's mother seemed more like a beautiful older sister in her speech, dress, and manner. Astonishing.

Sakanaka's stunning mother regarded Asahina's shrine-maiden-outfit-clad form curiously, laughing musically as she heard what occasioned our visit, and suggested that her daughter tended to spoil little Rousseau a bit too much. Haruhi, true to form, had no problem dealing with such an impressive lady, whereas I stood there stunned, feeling as though I should apologize for dirtying her beautiful home's entryway with my filthy feet.

Mrs. Sakanaka informed us that we would all be welcome to come inside when we returned, and somehow just at the right moment, Sakanaka herself emerged, having changed into normal clothes.

"Sorry to keep you waiting!"

I supposed one had to get dressed up for early spring walks around the neighborhood.

We left our things at the Sakanaka residence, and the six of us plus one dog left the house. Was I the only one who felt a little relieved? I wondered.

For some reason, it was Haruhi who wound up at the vanguard, holding Rousseau's leash as she headed straight out into the street.

"Okay, J.J., let's go!"

Just as I was feeling irritated at her persistent use of the nickname, she started trotting ahead. J.J. Rousseau seemed unworried by the fact that he'd only just met the person holding his leash, which made me wonder about dogs' reputations as humanity's constant watchful companions through the ages.

"Ah, Suzumiya, not that way! This is the route we walk, over here!"

Sakanaka was behind them, scoop and doggy bag in hand, and she stopped and waited for the smiling Haruhi to return. I was beginning to think these two made a good team.

Barring sickness or eccentricity, dogs generally love walks, and Rousseau had indeed inherited that proclivity. The little white dog trotted along, and trotting happily along behind him was Asahina, whose look alone made the scene seem like something out of a fantasy story.

Incidentally, since with Haruhi holding the leash she wouldn't have any idea where to go, somewhere along the way she handed it off to Sakanaka, behind whom the SOS Brigade formed up as we walked leisurely along.

"Which way is it? J.J., can't you run any faster? C'mon!" Haruhi tried to come alongside Rousseau and urge him along.

"It's too far for that, Suzumiya. We're going on a walk, not a run," answered Sakanaka mildly as Rousseau tugged on the leash.

Aside from Haruhi and her desire to run ahead and Asahina trailing single-mindedly behind the dog, Nagato was totally silent, and Koizumi had unfolded a city map.

I peered over at it. "What're you doing, looking at that? Are there sightseeing points around here or something?

When asked, Koizumi took a pen out of his pocket. "I was thinking of investigating places that are difficult for dogs to approach. Even if we can't walk to every single corner, once we have a vague idea of the territory, we should be able to figure out its shape on the map."

I decided to leave that to the diagram-lover here. Whether or not there actually was an area dogs refused to approach, just looking at the Sakanaka family dog's cheerful demeanor was enough to make me feel like I was out on an ordinary walk. I sort of wanted a dog of my own now. It didn't have to be one as fancy as this guy, though. I would be happy with a mutt. I looked at

Haruhi, and it seemed like she, too, had totally forgotten about all the ghost talk. She was just jumping around like a bunny, playing with Rousseau.

Our strange little group—all of us in our school uniforms save Sakanaka and one shrine maiden—faithfully traced the route of Rousseau's daily walk. Whether or not it was normal or strange, Sakanaka seemed quite serene as she walked along the path. It felt like we were heading east. If we kept heading this way, we'd encounter the river—the same cherry tree–lined river I'd thrown that turtle into, only to pick it back up and give it to the boy in glasses. It did have a walking path that would have been the perfect place to take your dog for a walk...

Just as I was contemplating it, Sakanaka came to an abrupt stop.

"Oh. Look, see, here's where he stops."

Rousseau had frozen in his tracks, feet firmly planted on the asphalt. Sakanaka tugged on his leash, but he resisted and backed away.

His owner wasn't the only person to heave a sigh of dismay at this end to our progress.

"Huh." Haruhi's eyes went wide as though she'd just remembered our real reason for being here. She surveyed the area. "This doesn't seem like a particularly suspicious area."

It was a residential neighborhood, but also close to the river, and greenery was plentiful. To the north, a mountain just about as high as North High's mountain was visible. There weren't bears around here, but I'd heard stories of wild boars occasionally coming down. But even so, it would be strange for them to appear in such a built-up area, and so near a train station; I'd never seen any news along those lines.

Sakanaka held the obstinate Rousseau's leash. "Up until last week I'd continue straight on ahead here, heading up the riverbank steps and walking along the path. After walking a while, I'd come back down the steps and come home. That was the route. But a week ago Rousseau started refusing to go near the river."

Asahina bent down and scratched the unmoving Rousseau's ears. Looking at the white, flicking points, Haruhi grabbed her own earlobe.

"Isn't the river pretty suspicious? Maybe it's been polluted with toxic waste. Maybe there's a chemical plant upstream or something!"

We North High students should know better than anyone else that there wasn't anything like that. If you followed this river upstream, you'd run smack into the route we took to and from school. There wasn't anything but mountains up there; it was deadly boring. It was so rural that there wasn't even anyplace decent to buy a snack.

"About that," said Sakanaka, explaining, "he doesn't mind heading farther up, nor farther downstream. Higuchi and Mrs. Anan said their dogs are the same way."

"Huh, interesting." Haruhi watched Rousseau lick the palm of Asahina's hand, then suddenly picked up the ball of fine white fur. "Okay, J.J.! You're gonna guide us around this area. When we get to a point you don't like, you just bark, got it? Here we go!"

Haruhi strode forcefully forward, but only got as far as the length of the leash held by Sakanaka—because the moment Rousseau had started to whine, his owner hadn't taken another step forward.

She looked every bit as sad and scared as Rousseau and obviously didn't want to see him traumatized. "I've never been angry with Rousseau," she said, taking him out of Haruhi's arms and stroking his head. "Did you know that there are dogs who die from the shock of their owners being angry at them? That's why."

I couldn't believe how dog-crazy she was. Even for the spoiled daughter of a rich family, there had to be limits to such things. I wanted to make her put up my Shamisen for a night. I'm sure it would've been like paradise for him.

Haruhi, too, gazed at Sakanaka in surprise, her mouth half open, but Asahina seemed to agree with this, nodding emphatically. I was a little jealous of the dog having managed to steal Asahina's heart so quickly.

"We weren't planning on forcing him *that* much," said Koizumi mildly as he cut into the conversation. The map fluttered in his hands. "Right now, we are"—he made a mark on the map in red pen—"here. The place from which dogs are sensing some sort of danger should be ahead of us. It should probably be considered an area rather than a point, but in any case, the farther we proceed, the harder it will be to narrow down the orientation of the phenomenon."

Before I could ask him what the hell he was talking about, Koizumi gave Sakanaka a smile, like a door-to-door salesman giving a hard sell.

"Let's head back for now. We'll let Rousseau lead the way, and he'll be able to enjoy a nice walk."

Just as Koizumi suggested, we headed back down the path we'd taken, and after about five minutes of walking, we took a left at an intersection and proceeded south. The closer we got to the train station, the more people there were. Fortunately, Asahina was more interested in Rousseau than in her own outfit, so she didn't seem too concerned about the looks she got from the passersby around us. Or maybe she'd just gotten used to going out in costume.

At the front of the group now was Koizumi, map in one hand. This was itself a fairly rare sight. He served as the trailblazer, handsome face, friendly smile, and all.

"This way next." Having initially directed us south, Koizumi now turned our little parade east.

And then, after another five minutes of walking, Rousseau began to whine again.

"Maybe it *is* the river?"

The direction Haruhi pointed was the direction we were all facing, from which we could see the slope of the riverbank's levee and the cherry trees that ran along it.

Once Koizumi established our exact location by checking some nearby addresses, he carefully marked our current spot on the map.

"And with this it starts to become clear. One more location should be enough."

I had no idea what was becoming clear to Koizumi, but we started heading south again. This time we didn't return to the street we'd taken to get here, rather taking a path that headed roughly toward the sea. Of course, we were nowhere near the actual sea, and it didn't seem as though Koizumi was planning to go that far; we'd only walked this way for about five minutes. We'd walked just about as far as we had from the place Rousseau first froze to our second stop, then headed east again.

This time it didn't even take three minutes.

*Whiiiine.*

For the third time, Rousseau refused to proceed. It was pretty sad, seeing the cute little stuffed animal–like dog get so upset, and I could understand why Sakanaka immediately scooped him up into her arms. It even got to me.

Asahina was agitated, Nagato was expressionless as ever, and Koizumi smiled cheerfully, as though satisfied. "I see," he said.

He put another mark on the map, then turned toward us as if to explain that the real challenge would start here. I fully expected him to say something incomprehensible again, but I couldn't very well keep ignoring him.

"What's going on?" He seemed to want me to ask, so I asked. I hoped he was grateful.

"Have a look at this map."

We all looked at the map Koizumi opened.

"The points marked in red are the points where Rousseau refused to continue. Including our position right now, there are three of them. Starting from the first one, we'll call them points A, B, and C. Looking at them, is there anything that jumps out at you?"

What, was he giving an open-air lecture now?

I'd given up on any academic study outside of a classroom, so I refused to answer the question, but Haruhi jumped on it without so much as raising her hand.

"The distances between A and B, and between B and C, are just about the same."

"Exactly so. That's why I chose this particular route," said Koizumi, satisfied at his model student. "The important concept to understand is that the individual points are not meaningful by themselves. Point B, in particular, is a mere checkpoint. Since evidence is better than theory, perhaps it would be easier to understand if I drew it."

Koizumi took the red pen and drew quickly on the map. It was a curve that led from A to C, with B as the midpoint. There was now a small arc on the 1:10,000-scale map.

"Oh, I see how it is." Haruhi seemed to have understood more quickly than anyone else. I had no idea.

"Kyon, don't you get it? What do you see in this curve?"

I didn't see anything other than a curve, I said.

"That's why you're so hopeless at math. You've got to understand this stuff intuitively. See? Koizumi, here—" Haruhi borrowed Koizumi's red pen and dropped a new line onto the map. "I'll extend the curve through the full sweep of its arc, and it makes a circle like this, see?"

Indeed it did. I was impressed at her ability to draw a nearly perfect circle freehand. It looked almost like the kind of mark you saw on a map that showed where the treasure was buried.

Oh. I finally understood. So that's how it was.

"You're saying that this circle is the area that dogs won't enter."

"It is merely a hypothesis," said Koizumi. "If the area is indeed circular, then we can hypothesize it thusly. While we have no way of knowing whether the cause is a supernatural phenomenon of some kind or some kind of harmful man-made substance, this does make it a bit easier to understand." He indicated the circle he and Haruhi had drawn. "If there is something here, the most suspicious point is the single place that's the same distance from every point on the circle—in other words, the center. With only three points of reference, there is a sizable margin of error, but not necessarily mistaken. And that puts the center—"

Haruhi, holding the pen, beat Koizumi's finger. "The riverbank!"

I didn't need Haruhi to say it. The center of the circle on the map was the cherry tree–lined path that was very familiar to me, directly opposite the bench I'd sat on and had that memorable conversation with Asahina.

"Wow!" said Sakanaka, impressed. "I'm amazed you could think of something like that, Koizumi!"

"It is nothing," said Koizumi with a smile.

Sakanaka looked keenly in his direction. I wanted to tell her she was better off staying away from him. You could never quite tell what he was thinking, plus he occasionally turned into a ball of glowing red energy.

I was about to warn her off, but I kept my mouth shut and continued to look at the map.

I got the feeling that every time something mysterious happened, I always seemed to find myself in familiar places. It was like I was being called there. I just hoped that this time I didn't have to save a boy from being run over or deal with some foul-mouthed new character showing up. Back then it had just been Asahina and me. But now the whole gang was here. There was no telling who would do what, especially Her Excellency the brigade chief.

"Let's go!" ordered Haruhi cheerfully. "To that mysterious spot. Sakanaka, J.J., you guys just relax and imagine you're on a pleasure cruise. Once we've taken pictures of the ghost or whatever it is, I'll be sure to exorcise it!"

"E-exorcise...?" Asahina hugged herself, apparently remembering what outfit she was wearing.

Haruhi grabbed her arm. "Now everyone, full-speed ahead!" she said, and took off running.

The spot in question was not far away, and we got there quickly thanks to Haruhi's forced march. The mystery spot indicated on Koizumi's map was right on the cherry tree–lined riverbank path, where the trees quietly gathered energy in preparation for their annual bloom.

Squinting at the map, Haruhi looked for the precise center, despite the fact that Koizumi's calculations had been fairly rough, making such precision pointless.

"Maybe around here?"

"This should be roughly the location."

In contrast to Haruhi's intent comparison of map with landscape, Koizumi's answer was vague.

Only the five full members of the SOS Brigade had come this far. Sakanaka and Rousseau retreated to their house—or rather, Sakanaka insisted that she "couldn't possibly force Rousseau to go somewhere he doesn't want to go," and declined to accompany us. Since the dog and the girl were useful only as witnesses, neither Haruhi nor I objected to this. Although, I must admit that if we're discussing utility, I myself was only worthwhile as an extra observer.

The one whose role was clearest was—

"Mikuru! Sorry to keep you waiting. It's your turn now!"

"O-Okay...!"

From Haruhi's perspective, Asahina was the only one to turn to now. That's why she'd forced the poor girl into that shrine-maiden outfit. If we turned around and headed home now, the costume would have been totally wasted.

"B-but, um...What should I...?"

"Don't sweat it! I've got everything ready. You just stand there, Mikuru. Right, and then hold this staff—"

Haruhi handed Mikuru a staff and made her take up a position in the grassy area near the river, then produced a rolled-up piece of copier paper from her skirt's pocket. "All right, now." Haruhi held the tremulous Asahina by the shoulders; Asahina looked beseechingly at the rest of us. "I don't see any obvious ghosts, so let's start the exorcism!"

"K-kanjizaibo...satsugyo...? Gyoujinhannyaa...haramiitajii... sh-shouken goun kaikuu...u..."

I was wondering what sort of "spell" Haruhi would come up with, but it was nothing—just the same Heart Sutra you could hear priests chanting at any Buddhist temple in Japan. I got the sense that the Shinto shrine maiden chanting a Buddhist sutra was sort of asking for trouble, but who was to say doubling up on religions wouldn't double the magical effectiveness of the ritual?

As she chanted, Asahina stared intently at the paper Haruhi had brought. I felt like I wanted to beg the forgiveness of the religious workers at every shrine and temple.

Haruhi continued to act as Asahina's assistant, flipping the phonetically transcribed pages of the Heart Sutra such that Asahina could keep reciting.

"D-d-doichi saiku yakushari...shikifu ikuukuu fuiishiki...?"

As Asahina continued to piously chant the sutra despite being a bogus shrine maiden, I took a look at the one person whose

reaction I was very interested in. I think it goes without saying who that was.

"..."

With eyes as clear as glass wind chimes ringing in the night air, Nagato gazed at Asahina from behind. She didn't look out of the ordinary, her slightly bored demeanor no different than usual. Her stillness was no different than when she was reading a book.

Maybe this meant I didn't have to worry.

I had no intention of saying there was something here at this precise point where Asahina was employing her chanting. But instead of looking for something occult right at this point, there might be something scientific affecting the area. However, if that were the case, there's no way Nagato wouldn't have noticed, and there's no way I wouldn't have noticed her noticing. By which I mean, she would have told me. Just like she had back during the cave-cricket incident.

Perhaps becoming aware of my looking at her, Nagato first moved her eyes, then her head to look at me, then made a short comment as though having read my mind.

"There is nothing."

No bombs or hibernating bears or atomic radiation sources or ancient coins—?

"No."

Not even a trace?

"Nothing within my capabilities to sense," said Nagato, as though she were reciting her times tables. "I detect no anomalous remnants."

So why did Rousseau and the other dogs refuse to come near this area? If there wasn't anything here, there was no reason for that.

"..."

Nagato moved her face like a wind chime stirred in a gentle breeze, looking diagonally past me.

I couldn't help following her gaze.

"Wha?"

A tall man in sportswear was jogging up from the river's downstream direction. I would've ignored him as a random jogger, but what drew my eye was the leash he held in one hand, the other end of which was attached to a collared dog. Not that a Shiba Inu was a particularly rare sight. It was a perfectly ordinary Shiba Inu.

But why was a dog here? Hadn't this area become a temporarily dog-free zone?

"Huh?" Haruhi seemed to have noticed. Asahina, too, lifted her eyes from the text and looked up, following our gazes and falling silent at their object.

"*Mucha muku... toku... Wha?*"

"Oh ho." Koizumi squinted at the dog running alongside the man.

The dog we were looking at had no trace of Sakanaka's West Highland White Terrier's reluctant conduct. It ran happily alongside its owner, panting steadily in its four-legged stride.

The young college-aged man and his dog regarded our far-more-suspicious group as he went to pass behind us, but then—

"Hey! Wait!" Haruhi jumped out and blocked his path. "We need to ask you something." She eyed the dog with her palpably keen, laser-like glare. "Can we have a minute of your time? Why can that dog run around here like normal? Ah, hmm, this might take a bit of time to explain," she said, then grabbed me by the tie and dragged me over. There, as the man looked on like he was wondering what our problem was, his dog's tongue lolling out as it watched us, Haruhi whispered into my ear. "C'mon, Kyon, you explain this."

Why did I have to do it?

Just as I was about to pass the baton to Koizumi, I found myself shoved by Haruhi in front of the dog and its master. Oh, well. I first apologized for disturbing his walk, then launched into the explanation. I told him that about a week ago, dogs had begun to refuse to enter this area. I explained that a friend of ours had asked us about it, and we'd thought it was suspicious enough to look into. That same dog had just minutes earlier refused to come near here. Just as we'd been sure we were close to finding something, he and his dog had come along, I told him. The clever-looking dog seemed perfectly happy, I said, but we didn't understand why.

"Oh, that," said the man of about twenty. He looked curiously at Asahina and her staff as he continued. "It's true that about a week ago, this guy," he said, pointing at the Shiba Inu, "started wanting to avoid our usual jogging course. When I'd try to get him up on the riverbank, he'd stop moving. I couldn't figure out why." The dog's athletic-looking master looked slowly between Asahina and Haruhi. "But this is the best road to walk him on, so I wondered if I could make him do it somehow. So the day before yesterday—or was it three days ago? Anyway, he really resisted at first, but as you can see, he's now happily running on his old course. He seems fine now."

I was no vet, but as far as I could tell, the well-mannered dog sitting at his master's feet was perfectly happy and the picture of health. He didn't seem worried about anything at all.

"I'll bet if your friend forced her dog a little bit, he'd be back to his old self. I don't know what the original cause was; maybe there was a bear or something, and its scent was lingering," said the man, echoing Koizumi's comment. "Will that be all?"

"Thank you very much. It really helped!" Haruhi honestly thanked him.

The young man looked at Asahina's outfit, seeming for a moment like he wanted to say something, but perhaps he wasn't the nosy type. We were lucky he was so nice. "'Bye," he said, and jogged on upriver.

Left behind were five dunderheads: me, Haruhi holding the

sutra, Asahina looking like she'd gotten lost on the way to the local shrine, Nagato watching the river flow by, and Koizumi stroking his chin thoughtfully.

"So what does this mean?"

It meant just what we'd seen and heard, I said.

"What about the ghost? I was really looking forward to that."

Shouldn't she be admitting there wasn't one all along?

So what was happening?

Heck if I knew.

"...You seem weirdly happy. It bugs me."

That wasn't fair. I always tried to keep a straight face. It wasn't as though I was deeply relieved that her expectations hadn't been fulfilled, and that whatever was here was now long gone, I said.

"Liar."

Haruhi turned on her heel and walked away from me, her strides long and quick.

We put the tree-lined riverside path behind us and headed to rendezvous with Sakanaka at her house. We'd left our bags there, and we needed to deliver our report to the client.

"But, um..." Diagonally behind me walked Asahina, who spoke in a hesitant voice. "But I really wonder what was going on. Even today, Rousseau didn't want to walk that way."

Koizumi jumped on this. "According to the fellow we just talked to, it was three days ago that he solved the problem. We know that there was definitely something alarming dogs until that point. But now it seems there is not. The fact that according to Sakanaka, other neighborhood dogs won't approach the area—it is probably because their memories are still making them sense danger. If that Shiba Inu's master hadn't forced him back onto the path, he probably wouldn't have come near it."

Weren't there two kinds of dogs? Those who excelled at remembering difficult events and those who didn't? Upon reflection,

Rousseau was on the smart side of things, and that Shiba Inu had a pretty good brain too.

"..."

I felt better seeing Nagato remaining silent. If she said there wasn't anything here, then there definitely wasn't anything here. At the moment, I didn't care that someone had tossed his vote in favor of the theory of a hibernating bear having left the area and returned to the mountain three days ago.

It was still the time of year when the air becomes chilly at dusk, and Haruhi's pace brought us quickly to the Sakanaka mansion. Perhaps it wounded our brigade chief's pride to have to tell a rare client that we hadn't been able to figure anything out, since she was rather irritable, but knowing her personality, she'd soon recover. It was Haruhi Suzumiya's habit not to spend time worrying about things that don't work out, instead moving on to the next adventure.

As expected, Haruhi's mood immediately improved upon arriving at the Sakanaka residence, where we were invited into the living room and served handmade *choux à la crème* pastries.

"Whoa. Yum. These are tasty. You could open a shop with these!"

The living room's furnishings were chic and tasteful, and the sofa I sat on was so fluffy that if Shamisen got on it, he'd probably sleep for twelve hours straight. The beautiful Mrs. Sakanaka's dog was even high-class—everything from the appearance to the aura of a wealthy person's home was just different. I wondered if Haruhi's personality would've been closer to Sakanaka's if she'd been raised in this kind of environment.

While we were partaking of *choux à la crème* and Earl Grey tea, Koizumi related the details of our investigation. Sakanaka held Rousseau and stroked his head while nodding in response to the report. However, when the explanation was over, she seemed to still find something puzzling.

"I understand that it seems safe now," she said, looking at Rousseau's alert ears, "but seeing how scared Rousseau got earlier, I don't think I'll make him walk that path until he and the other neighborhood dogs don't mind it anymore. I'd feel bad for him otherwise."

That was certainly her decision to make as the dog owner. Rousseau was lucky to have such a considerate caretaker, although it seemed to me she spoiled him a little too much.

Delighted at Haruhi's and Nagato's devouring of her *choux à la crème*, Mrs. Sakanaka was busily making more, and for a while the topic was dominated by Sakanaka's tales of her dog. Rousseau himself was lying on his belly beside Sakanaka, ears initially pricked and alert, but eventually his eyes began to look sleepy. Asahina adoringly watched him, a wistful sigh escaping her lips.

"You're so lucky to have a dog…"

I wondered if pets were banned in the future, but to be perfectly honest, I'd take Asahina in my house over a pet any day. Having a maid to see me off in the morning and welcome me home—was that not the proper job of a maid? It certainly suited her better than brewing tea in a dingy clubroom.

Oh, well. I'd just leave that one in the world of my thoughts.

The day ended with us having all gone to Sakanaka's house, playing with her dog, going on a walk, having Asahina dressed as a shrine maiden and chanting the Heart Sutra, taking *choux à la crème* and tea, then going home—just a normal day having fun with a classmate.

And what I expected would happen was that the mystery would go unsolved, disappearing from my memory as well as Haruhi's…

But a few days later, something unexpected happened.

It was Friday. The school-wide sports tournament as well as final exams had come to an end, so the last thing the first-year high school students had to do was wait for spring break to start while worrying about what their class assignments would be for the next year. The graduation ceremony had happened at the end of February, and with a third of the student body gone, the school buildings were somehow quiet, although come next month they'd be filled again with fresh-faced new students, just as we ourselves had once done.

Was I now going to be called "senpai"? It was hard to imagine the SOS Brigade getting any new members, but what were Haruhi's plans?

Sitting in the second seat from the back in the row against the windows, I yawned widely and stretched in the rays of spring sunshine that shone through.

"Kyon." Someone sitting in the seat behind me, the last one in the row, poked me in the back with a mechanical pencil.

"What?" If she wanted me to try and persuade incoming freshmen to join, she could forget about it, I said.

"That's not it. That's my job, anyway. But whatever." Haruhi gestured to the rest of the classroom with the point of her pencil. "Did you notice that Sakanaka was absent today?"

"No... Was she?"

"She was. She's been gone since this morning."

That was surprising. Aside from pointing out how stupid Taniguchi was, the only time Haruhi'd ever said anything about one of our classmates was during the Asakura incident, I pointed out.

"Well, we had her as a client, so I was going to ask whether her dog-walking route had returned to normal. Don't you care? Plus, the dog was cute and those cream puffs were delicious. I'm not *that* forgetful, you know."

Normally I would've been delighted to hear that Haruhi had finally become good enough friends with a girl in the class that she cared about where she was, but now that she mentioned it, it did bother me. After all, it was undeniably true that there was an area near Sakanaka's house where her dog would refuse to go, and that being the case, we'd left the matter unresolved. But now she was absent from school. It wasn't inconceivable that there was a connection, but—

"Well, the seasons are changing. Maybe she caught a cold. And it *is* the end of the semester, after all. If she's ditching, it's not that big of a deal."

"Maybe." Happily, Haruhi agreed. "I guess if I didn't have the SOS Brigade, I wouldn't see any use in coming to school now. But Sakanaka seems too serious to just up and turn a normal weekday into a holiday on her calendar."

Given that Haruhi was constantly taking holidays and making them into SOS Brigade activities, I wouldn't have expected her to be so particular about sticking to the calendar.

"Mmm." Haruhi held her pencil between her nose and upper lip. "Maybe we should go investigate again. I'll have Mikuru wear a nurse outfit this time."

Having her wear a nurse outfit without having any actual credentials was only going to cause trouble, I pointed out. And wasn't she just after more *choux à la crème*?

"Idiot. I want to see J.J. Don't you wonder what would happen if you sheared that wool-like fur off of him?"

Bored, Haruhi began spinning her pencil around her fingertips, as the bell signaling the beginning of third period rang.

After school, things started moving all at once.

I was in the clubroom playing shogi against Koizumi, Nagato was reading, and Asahina was busy making tea, wearing the maid outfit that suited her much better than the shrine-maiden one did.

Then—Haruhi barged in the room, having been delayed by classroom cleaning duties.

"Kyon, I knew it!"

Normally when she made these sorts of pronouncements, Haruhi was smiling, but that day she seemed vaguely melancholy. I had a premonition that strange things were happening.

"I figured out why Sakanaka is absent. She's fine, but it's Rousseau—he's been taken to an animal hospital. But even the vet doesn't know what's wrong with him, so she's really depressed. She was so upset she couldn't come to school! I talked to her on the phone, and she sounded like she was about to cry. Her stomach's been hurting so badly she hasn't eaten anything, but since Rousseau isn't eating either, it just makes her feel worse—"

"Hang on, calm down," was all I could think of to say, but interrupting Haruhi in the middle of her sentence only got me a harsh glare—not angry, exactly, but as though I was a heartless bastard who'd abandoned a drowning child.

"What's your problem? You're just sitting there drinking tea while Rousseau's in agony! J.J.'s so weak he can't even drink water!"

If drinking tea were now a crime, then Koizumi and Asahina were my accomplices, but in any case, I wanted her to tell me just how she'd already known the circumstances in the Sakanaka household by the time she'd come barging into the room.

"I called Sakanaka's cell phone while I was cleaning. I was just really worried about her. And then—"

That was the second surprise of the day. Since when had Haruhi been good enough friends with Sakanaka to trade cell phone numbers?

"—I knew it wasn't any time to mess around with cleaning!" Haruhi brandished her cell phone. "There *was* something in that area. What I think is that whatever's there is the cause of the sickness. I mean, Sakanaka said it herself. Other dogs in the area have been affected too."

I'd heard that part too; I remembered it as soon as Haruhi mentioned it.

"If the symptoms are the same, then maybe…"

"The symptoms *are* the same," said Haruhi flatly. "I asked her about it. She said when she went to the animal hospital, the vet said they'd gotten a similar case in a few days earlier. When she asked about it, it turned out it was Higuchi's dog."

Who was this Higuchi?

"Geez, Kyon, you're so stupid! Sakanaka told us about her before. Higuchi, who has a bunch of dogs! She lives close to the Sakanaka house. Didn't you hear that one of them wasn't feeling well?"

Yeah, I'd just now remembered, I told her. I bet she'd forgotten all about it too until she called; it wasn't fair that she was attacking me for it. But anyway—Rousseau was sick? He'd been so healthy.

"What's he sick with?" I asked.

"They don't know, she said." Haruhi just stood there, as though she'd forgotten to sit at her brigade chief's desk. "Apparently it's got the vet totally stumped. There's nothing wrong with his body, his health is just failing, and Higuchi's Mike is the same way. They've just lost their appetites and collapsed. He's not barking or sniffing and Sakanaka's getting more and more worried."

Haruhi glared as me as though it were my fault, then looked over the other occupants of the clubroom.

Asahina clasped her serving tray, looking stricken from worry about Rousseau. Nagato looked up from her book to Haruhi. Koizumi put the shogi piece in his hand back from where he had picked it up and spoke.

"It seems we'll need to reinvestigate the area," he said with a smile like a veterinarian encouraging a worried pet owner. "This is, after all, a case brought to us by Sakanaka. We cannot shut our eyes to this. You could say it's our duty to see it through to the end."

"Th-that's right. We should go visit them at the hospital." Asahina nodded her agreement with Koizumi's stance.

"..."

Nagato closed her book and silently stood.

The entire brigade seemed to be united in its worry about Rousseau. The dog had frightening charisma to have inspired such concern in all of them over only a day's worth of activity.

"What about you?" Haruhi glared at me, accusation in her eyes. "What's it gonna be?"

Naturally I felt badly about the fluffy little guy being in bad shape. Unlike, say, Shamisen, he was a purebred terrier from Scotland, raised in a comfortable home his whole life—he probably wasn't that tough.

And that aside, I was worried about the unknown cause of this affliction. I looked away from Haruhi to avoid her glare, my eyes fixing upon another person.

"..."

Yuki Nagato, who'd promised that there wasn't anything out of the ordinary at that location, was in the middle of picking up her book bag.

After a bit of time spent waiting for Asahina to change clothes, we headed out of school, walking as fast as we could down the hill and catching a train that was literally on the verge of departing toward Sakanaka's house. Having commenced her action, Haruhi's mobility and command were greater than any commander in the Mongolian horde.

We arrived shortly at the expensive neighborhood, and when we got to the house, I watched Haruhi's finger as she pressed the doorbell button.

"Coming..."

When Sakanaka emerged, it was obvious by looking at her that she was totally dispirited. Her face was weary, and her eyes were moist from recently crying.

"Come in. Suzumiya, everybody...thank you so much for..."

Her words trailed off as she beckoned us in, toward the living room we'd been in before. There on the fine couch, probably in Sakanaka's own personal spot, was Rousseau, his legs drawn in beneath him as he lay there. His white fur seemed to have lost its luster, and he rested his head on the sofa's cushion, evidently too exhausted even to look up at the large group of people that had just entered the room. His ears didn't so much as twitch.

"Rousseau..." Asahina immediately approached him, kneeling down and stroking his nose. His little black eyes moved, looking sadly up at Asahina, then shifted slowly away. Asahina laid the palm of her hand on Rousseau, but all he did was reflexively move his ears slightly. Whatever his affliction, it was definitely serious.

"How long has he been like this?" Haruhi asked.

Sakanaka's voice was strained. "Probably since yesterday evening. I thought he was just sleepy, so I didn't worry about it at the time, but when I woke up in the morning, he was still the same way. He won't move from this spot, and he won't eat. He couldn't do his morning walk either. I got worried so I took him to the animal hospital, but..."

So everything Haruhi had been shouting about in the clubroom was true—that the cause was unknown, and that there was another dog with a similar problem, I said.

"Yes. Higuchi's dog Mike. He's a miniature dachshund and good friends with Rousseau."

Asahina stroked Rousseau's head sympathetically, with the special kindness of someone who believes that small animals must be treasured. Her sadness at Rousseau's condition was obvious even to me, and as I tried to prevail over the sudden tightness in my chest—

"May I ask something?" said Koizumi. "If that's the case, then Higuchi's Mike should have been affected five days ago. What is Mike's condition now?"

"I called around noon today. He said Mike's been bad for days and still is. Since he won't eat, he was put on an IV to get some nutrients into his body. I don't know what I'm going to do if they have to do that to Rousseau..."

If things kept up this way, he'd just keep getting weaker. I thought about the difference between the images of the healthy, happy dog I'd seen just a few days before and the one I saw now. He suddenly reminded me of the way Shamisen would lie lethargically on the heater, but this was a dog, so his circumstances were different. I was starting to get genuinely worried.

"One more thing," said Koizumi. "Is it just Mike and Rousseau who've been affected? I believe you said there are many dogs that Rousseau goes on walks with."

"I haven't heard if anyone else is like this. When Mike got sick, there were a lot of rumors about it, so if other dogs are sick, I'm sure I would have heard about it."

"And this Mike, is the owner's residence nearby?"

"Yes. It's across the street, just three doors down. What about it?"

"Oh, nothing." Koizumi ended his questioning.

Wilting, Sakanaka said, "I wonder if it really is a ghost. I mean, the vet at the animal hospital couldn't figure it out..."

Haruhi furrowed her brow, her voice small and desperate. "Maybe...It *is* strange, isn't it? Whether or not it's a ghost, it's sure no laughing matter."

Her expression made it seem like she was regretting jumping so quickly on the idea of a ghost, dressing Asahina up as a shrine maiden and making her chant sutras. It seemed like she was thinking ruefully that a real vengeful spirit was going to take more than a costume to beat. For Haruhi, it was a serious regret.

"Hey, Yuki, can't you do something?"

It was strange that she'd suddenly ask Nagato, but in response, the quiet girl naturally took action. She set down her book bag and moved toward Rousseau, kneeling down in the space beside the worried Asahina and looking directly into the dog's eyes.

I held my breath and looked on.

"..."

Nagato slipped her finger beneath Rousseau's chin and lifted up his head, looking steadily into Rousseau's black eyes. Her eyes were even and serious, like lasers reading data directly from the surface of a DVD. Their noses were so close they were almost touching as Nagato gazed into Rousseau's eyes, which she did for about thirty seconds.

"..."

She stood up slowly, seeming almost more ghostly than an actual ghost, and we all watched as she walked back to her original place in the room, and slowly, minutely cocked her head.

Haruhi sighed.

"You don't know either, Yuki? I guess that's natural. Hmm..."

I don't know what I expected from Nagato, but evidently treating this problem was beyond the scope of Nagato's considerable power. I supposed even aliens weren't gods, and I slumped in discouragement—when from behind me I felt a strong presence.

I looked back. Nagato was staring at me, and after a brief moment, she nodded so imperceptibly, I doubted it was detectable on the micrometer scale. She then looked away.

Nobody should've noticed. Haruhi, Asahina, Sakanaka, and even Nagato were all focused on the exhausted Rousseau. But one sharp-eyed person had noticed Nagato's actions.

"I believe we should retreat for the moment," whispered Koizumi into my ear. "There's nothing we can do by remaining here. Not you and not me." Koizumi smiled quietly, then spoke again. I didn't like him breathing on me. It felt weird. "There's no hurry, but we mustn't waste time. If nothing else, there's Suzumiya's state to consider. We need to deal with this before she takes some kind of disastrous action. And the only person who can do that is—"

I wanted to play dumb and ask him what the hell he was getting at, but for some reason, I knew exactly what he was talking about. Maybe I'm naturally smart. I didn't know why it was so easy for me to read Nagato's and Koizumi's every tiny expression and still be so hopeless at exams, but this was no time to be worrying about that. And this wasn't for Koizumi's sake; this was for Rousseau.

It was time to get things done.

Having left Sakanaka's house, Haruhi and Asahina were listless and absent, as though they'd left their souls back with the poor sick dog, and they remained silent on the train. Even when we got off at our station, it was like Sakanaka had been contagious and they'd caught her sadness.

As far as that went, I understood it perfectly well. It was hard seeing someone who'd once been healthy losing that health. I, too, wanted to see them running around the school, not lost in melancholy. Whether it was a person or an animal.

But it was Koizumi's cold conclusion that as far as the dog went, there was currently nothing we laypeople could do for it.

"All we can do is watch and wait. But the animal hospital is not powerless. I expect even now they're working on a treatment."

I just hoped it was a sickness that could be researched and understood. But what if it wasn't? I didn't want to have to go to Rousseau's funeral, I said.

"Fortunately, I know some veterinarians. I'll do some asking around; they may have some leads."

In spite of Koizumi's forced attempt to cheer them up, Haruhi and Asahina had lukewarm reactions. All he got from them were murmured *yeah*s and *okay*s.

We couldn't very well sit around stewing in our own sadness forever, so eventually we decided to call it a day. Or should I say, we *had* to. If we hadn't, who knows for how long we would've wound up staring dejectedly into space.

Haruhi and Asahina walked side-by-side down the road that paralleled the train tracks. By rights, Koizumi and I would've taken the same route, since it was the quickest way for us to get home, but Haruhi didn't seem to notice our absence, and the two of them were soon out of sight.

I hate to say it, but they were in the way. It would've been nice if Asahina could have stayed, but the current situation was not her specialty.

Along with Koizumi and me, Nagato watched the two girls head home, then turned to return to her own apartment.

"Nagato."

The small, short-haired girl looked back mechanically, smoothly, as though she'd expected me to call her name.

I saw her face and had a hunch. I knew it. Nagato *did* understand. I didn't have to hesitate to ask her.

"What is it that Rousseau's gotten?"

I wondered if she was going to think about it for a moment, but then Nagato spoke.

"A data life-form element."

To that statement, I said:

"…"

Perhaps recognizing my silence as noncomprehension, Nagato amended her explanation. "A silicon-based, symbiotic data life-form element."

"…"

In response to my continuing silence, Nagato opened her mouth to explain further, but then seemed to realize she had no other words of explanation, and so closed it.

While the two of us fell silent, Koizumi spoke.

"In other words, Rousseau has been infected by an invisible extraterrestrial life-form," he offered.

Nagato seemed to pause for a moment, as though waiting for permission from someone. Then: "Yes." She nodded.

"I see. So this data life-form element—may we consider it not as being invisible to the human eye, but rather having no physical form at all, instead being comprised of pure data?"

"You may."

"Is it similar to the Data Overmind in that regard? Like the network infection that spread to the computer club president?"

"The Data Overmind is on a completely different level from this subspecies. It is far more primitive."

"Are there any comparisons at all? If you compare the Data Overmind to a human, then what would be analogous to this silicon-based, symbiotic data life-form element?"

I was shocked he'd been able to remember that term, having only heard it once. In response to Koizumi's question barrage, Nagato answered the same way she always did: simply.

"A virus."

"Is that it, then? Is the reason the first dog's body...no, its mind was infected, before the infection was passed on to Rousseau, because the data life-form elements are reproducing and spreading, like a virus?" Koizumi brushed a lock of hair back with his finger. "And what are these strange data life-forms doing on Earth? And what attracted them to the dogs?"

"It is possible," said Nagato in a thin voice, "to surmise that the silicate bodies that act as hosts were drawn into Earth's gravity well. Those silicate bodies were vaporized by the heat from atmospheric friction, but data life-forms can continue to exist when the physical matter that houses them is destroyed. The data remains. The data life-form elements made contact with the Earth's surface."

"Right where the dogs are being walked. That's the area where they fell, is it not? And they happened to infect a dog that passed by."

"It is possible that there are similarities between the networks of silicon-based life-forms and canine neural circuitry."

"But they're not the same. Which means the result is that the dogs begin to weaken."

Nagato had been answering Koizumi's questions rapidly, but she closed her mouth for a moment to consider.

"It is not a contagion. A unified data element is planning to expand its cognitive memory."

What was she talking about—

Whatever it was, Koizumi seemed to understand. "So a single dog doesn't contain sufficient resources. But I can't imagine it will stop, having spread to two dogs. How many dogs would it take for this silicon-based life-form to rebuild its network?"

"Based on the minimum estimate derived from silicon life-forms already known to my database...infecting every dog on the planet would be insufficient—"

"Now wait just a second," I interrupted, deeply disturbed. "I understand that Rousseau and one other dog have gotten some kind of space virus. And I kind of get that it got here on a meteorite. But what—in space, there are these...uh, how did you put it, Nagato, 'organic life-forms,' but also other life-forms, ones not made out of organic matter?"

Nagato considered her answer for a moment. "The answer to that question depends on how you define the concept of life." She looked at me with eyes so clear I thought I might fall into them. "If you are referring to entities whose consciousnesses are contained within silicate constructions, such entities exist."

She said it like it was no big deal, but hearing something so intense at this particular moment put me in a bad place. She should've told the Project Cyclops extraterrestrial investigators when they were putting together SETI; they would've done a happy dance and run off to get funding, I bet.

"And by the way," I said, even though it was a little late to ask, "what's this 'silicon' you keep talking about?"

Unfortunately I'd never been overly fond of either chemistry class or its teacher.

"It's the chemical element, silicon," said Koizumi. "It's an excellent semiconductor." He directed an interested smile at Nagato. "What Nagato is talking about is essentially a machine consciousness. It's a level of technology we humans have not yet achieved. She's saying that elsewhere in the universe, there are inorganic, machine entities that have gained consciousness on their own. Or perhaps in all of space, such entities are the norm, and we humans are the exception."

Nagato ignored Koizumi and kept looking at me. As though she were entrusting me with the answer to everything.

I thought back—back to the first book I'd borrowed from Nagato. Guided by a note left on a bookmark in it, I'd gone to her house for the first time, where she'd told me something.

—*Because it was previously assumed that organic life-forms, which possess absolute limits on their data accumulation and transmission capabilities, could never develop intelligence*—

Koizumi unconsciously stroked his chin.

"Is it possible that these silicon compositions are merely raw matter, and only gained consciousness upon being inhabited by the data elements?"

Nagato looked up, seeming again as though she were asking someone for permission, then looked back down.

"Intelligence," she said after a short pause, "is determined by an entity's ability to collect data, then independently process that stored data."

Nagato was very talkative—no, more talkative than she'd been since the conversation in which she'd revealed her true nature to me. Maybe the fact that our problem was in her area of expertise made her chattier.

"The data life-form element parasitizes the silicon life-forms, augmenting their cognitive abilities. Originally the data life-form was no more than an isolated clump of information. In order to harvest and process more data, it required physical network circuitry. Each entity benefits the other."

But what were these silicon-based life-forms? Were they so astoundingly lazy and disconnected that they'd just let themselves fall into Earth's gravity well and burned up in the atmosphere? I asked.

"Their activities as life-forms are limited to cognition," said Nagato. "They do nothing other than cogitate. Space is vast. The probability that they would fall into a gravity well is near zero. Thus they have no will to live nor self-preservation concepts."

What did they think about, just floating around in space? I asked.

"It is impossible to explain their cognitive framework to an organic life-form. Their logical foundations are too different."

So communication was impossible, huh. I guess we didn't have to alert NASA then. Making first contact would only end in frustration.

"Geez."

We'd gone from Sakanaka talking about ghosts to the far reaches of the universe—a leap too far, if you asked me. And given that I could barely understand any of Nagato's hard SF novels, all this talk of intelligence and cognitive capability was totally beyond me.

It was hard to know whether it fell in the purview of chemistry, philosophy, or religion. Invisible data life-forms and the intelligent balls of silicon that housed them...it would've been a lot more understandable to just call them ghosts and be done with it.

"Wait—," I said, as something weird occurred to me. That's right—Sakanaka had come to us talking about ghosts. And a ghost was just a soul, right? "So, do souls exist?"

This formless data life-element, or whatever it was, was the source of extraterrestrial intelligence. Its former physical body had been destroyed, and its incorporeal part had fallen to Earth—didn't that make it basically a ghost?

"What about humans? We have brains that think, which means there's a consciousness in there somewhere. Are you saying even if our body is destroyed, the spirit remains?"

This was a fairly important question—no, there was no "fairly" about it. Depending on the answer, it could completely change the path of a human life.

Nagato did not answer, a queer look passing across her face. I mean, her standard lack of expression was the same as ever, but something about her aura was different, I could tell. Even if nobody else noticed, I could tell. I would soon have known her for an entire year. That was plenty of time to develop a certain amount of insight, and there'd been several incidents where it would've been impossible *not* to learn something about her. Trust me, I'd know.

Nagato, she—

"..."

She was silent, she was blank, and yet I felt that there was some kind of a look to her. And so long as my perception wasn't indicating "zero"—

"..."

It was like she was trying to avoid smiling at her own joke.

Then, finally, Nagato's answer came. It was short and sweet.

"That is classified."

There was a loud, exaggerated sigh. I was its source. Classified, huh? Someday I wanted to be able to use that word when somebody had asked me a question I didn't want to answer. Maybe I'd try it in class the next time a teacher put me on the spot.

I was struck by the deep question of whether Nagato had just cracked the first joke she'd ever made in her entire life, but that wasn't important. Right now, Rousseau was the top priority. The problem was what to do about that space-virus thing.

"We'll have to do something. Nagato, is it possible?"

"It is possible," said Nagato. You could always count on her. "We must gain control of the relevant data life-form elements and compress them into an archive, halting its activity. However, we will need a biological network to contain the archived data."

I didn't really understand, but it sounded like a pain. Couldn't we just wipe it out? I asked.

"Deletion is not possible."

Why not?

"Permission has not been given."

From her boss?

"Yes."

Had they been designated an endangered species in this galaxy or something?

"It is a beneficial being."

I supposed they were something like *lactobacilli* or *E. coli* to us humans, then.

I'd let Koizumi take over. He seemed amused at something. "Can't we stick this thing in some silicon and send it back to space in a rocket or something? Couldn't your Agency handle something like that?"

Koizumi shrugged lightly. "I could get as many ingots as you want from Silicon Valley, and it wouldn't be impossible to manipulate political and economic conditions to get access to a hydrogen rocket, but it doesn't seem likely that we'll be able to prepare silicon-based life-forms."

No good, huh? No...wait.

In my mind appeared an image of a beautifully patterned metal rod. It was a Genroku-era relic that had been excavated from Tsuruya's mountain, which the family had then put in storage. Had it been prepared for the eventuality we now faced? Was this out-of-place artifact a gift from the past?

"No, it's not."

According to what Tsuruya had said, the metal rod in the picture was composed of a titanium-cesium alloy. If news of it reached the academic world, they'd have something crazier to debate than the location of the Yamatai Kingdom, but it was unrelated to some bone-dry, fossilized silicon life-form. It was part of some other machine, or was something that had to be sealed away for eternity, or had been left by some traveler from the future. I never wanted to see it again, if I could avoid it, even if I *had* been the reason it had been discovered.

I was lost in my own musing when Koizumi's voice brought me back around.

"Fortunately, it does not seem as though haste is necessary. There were several days between the first dog's health failing and Rousseau being affected. If we can do something about it today or tomorrow, we should be able to avoid having any other victims."

There was a huge difference in the time scales here on Earth, compared with the cosmos. I supposed I should be grateful that this virus thing seemed to have stayed on cosmic time.

"We'll visit Sakanaka again tomorrow. There's no school. But we should think hard about the reason for our visit. It may not be strange to check in on the dog's health two days running, but we're actually going to treat it. And we'll need to do the same thing with Higuchi's dog too."

I was only half listening to Koizumi. I didn't care if he couldn't think of a pretext. Nagato was going to be the one doing the actual treatment.

"Tomorrow, then. Sorry, Nagato—we're gonna be counting on you."

Not unlike the way Haruhi and Asahina had left their hearts at Sakanaka's house, I couldn't stop my own heart from flying out into the cosmos. I was totally spaced out, and as I went to leave, something slowed my exiting body. What the?

I looked behind me. Nagato had grabbed my belt and stopped me. I didn't really mind, but she should've raised her voice, or at least tugged on my sleeve or something. Come to think of it, I would've preferred the latter.

Her face blank, Nagato moved her lips and spoke. "There is something we need."

"What?"

"A cat."

I was totally taken aback; Nagato spoke as if choosing her words carefully.

"The cat at your house would be ideal."

A little while after Koizumi, Nagato, and I had finished strategizing, I made a phone call as I walked home.

"Haruhi? Yeah, it's me. I want to talk about Rousseau. She was talking about this on the way back, but it turns out that Nagato once read a book that had a dog with a sickness a lot like Rousseau's...Yeah, the treatment was in there too. I can't say for sure it'll go well, but...yeah, I know. It's worth trying, right? Nagato knows how to do it. So tomorrow we're going to go back to Sakanaka's place and...what, now? Can't do it. There's stuff to get ready, so we'll meet up tomorrow. Don't rush things. According to Koizum—I mean, Nagato—it's not something that's going to suddenly get worse...Yeah, why don't you go ahead and tell Sakanaka. Oh, and there was another dog, right? Higuchi's dog Mike or whatever. They'll need to bring him over to Sakanaka's place too. I'll tell Asahina. Okay, see you tomorrow.... Yeah, nine o'clock. Okay? At the usual station."

The next day, at the station that would any day now turn into a famous sightseeing destination, I arrived twenty minutes early only to discover the rest of the brigade waiting for me.

However, only Koizumi and Nagato looked anything like their usual selves; Asahina stood there, unease on her face, while Haruhi looked like someone who'd put all her money into the lottery and was waiting for the numbers to be announced.

"You're late." She glared at me with a complicated expression.

That day, for once, I wasn't made to treat the rest of the brigade at the café as a tardiness punishment. Haruhi just grabbed my arm and started walking toward the ticket machines.

"I heard more about it from Koizumi," she said as she bought tickets for all of us. "That Nagato's going to try some kind of folk remedy? For something called 'suncat'?"

*Suncat?* What was that supposed to be? It sounded like a new kind of fairy from Polynesia or something.

"It's the illness we believe Rousseau has contracted." Having gotten his ticket, Koizumi reached out to the automatic turnstile. He quickly continued, perhaps to stop me from contradicting the story he'd come up with. "When an otherwise active dog suddenly loses all of his energy and acts like a cat sleeping in a sunbeam, it indicates a case of this disease. It's an extremely rare affliction and is not in any veterinary manuals. There's a possibility it's a sort of neurosis," he said, winking at me, "or so Nagato has explained it to me. Evidently she learned about it in some old book. Isn't that right?"

Nagato, the only one of us still wearing her school uniform, nodded plainly enough for everyone to see. The nod was so awkward that it was painfully obvious they'd discussed this ahead of time.

She looked at the paper supermarket bag that Koizumi held, then regarded the pet carrier I was holding.

"*Meow*," said Shamisen, as if to greet Nagato, scratching at the holes in the box he was in.

Haruhi *thwack*ed the cat carrier. "It's so weird to need a cat to treat a disease. Yuki, are you sure this is okay? Can we trust that book?"

It was a lot closer to an exorcism than a treatment, but we couldn't very well tell that to Haruhi. I was glad for Nagato's policy of silence.

She nodded, then, turning her head to regard me, held out both hands. Just when I was wondering what she wanted, since all I had was this cat in a plastic box, she spoke.

"The cat," said Nagato, her voice flat. "Give it to me."

Thus I became empty-handed, and while the carrier box containing the cat was on the train, it rested on Nagato's lap. Maybe because we were on a train, I couldn't tell if the silent girl was trying to give me some kind of a sign, but Shamisen behaved himself.

Haruhi and Asahina sat on either side of Nagato, and in contrast to their interest in the cat-filled box, I was much more interested in the contents of Koizumi's bag.

"Don't worry; I've prepared suitable tools."

The two of us boys were leaning against the door of the train car, so there was no concern that Haruhi would overhear our conversation. Koizumi moved the bag slightly.

"It took a bit of effort getting it ready in a single night, but I managed. The rest is up to Nagato."

I had no doubts about Nagato's abilities. She would save Rousseau. What was giving me a headache was thinking about cleaning up afterward.

"That'll be my job. This is just my intuition, but I don't think this will be too troublesome. You'll see if you watch Suzumiya. Her highest priority right now is to cure Rousseau. So long as we can accomplish that, we'll have fulfilled our duties."

I hoped he was right.

I took my eyes off the unconcernedly smiling Koizumi and grabbed a handhold as the train began to decelerate. There were only two more stations to Sakanaka's neighborhood. There wasn't much time left to think.

This made it the third day we'd visited Sakanaka's house. I would never have imagined we'd be coming here three times in a single week.

Sakanaka met us at the door, looking much the same as she had the previous day, though her eyes were colored by what might have been a sliver of hope.

"Suzumiya..." She seemed on the verge of tears and at a loss for words; Haruhi simply nodded and looked back. She was searching for the best and brightest member of the SOS Brigade—the slender, school-uniformed Nagato.

"Leave it to us, Sakanaka. You might not think it, but Yuki's super dependable, and she can do practically anything. J.J. will be better before you know it."

We were led shortly into the Sakanakas' living room, where there was Mrs. Sakanaka along with another woman. Something about her said "ladies' college student" to me, and no sooner did I look at her face than I understood she was Higuchi, owner of the other afflicted dog. Which meant that the exhausted miniature dachshund she held in her arms had to be Mike.

Rousseau was much the same as he had been the previous day, lying on the couch, motionless. His eyes were open, but he didn't seem to be looking at anything, and Mike was exactly of a kind.

This was it. I exchanged looks with Nagato and Koizumi.

I began taking brief instructions from Nagato, acting as her assistant, just as the three of us had decided at our last meeting. Koizumi had brought the appropriate tools. I didn't know where he'd gotten them, but I had to admit, the guy was pretty useful in times like this. It was a lot easier than trying to get our hands on a silicon-based life-form.

First we closed the curtains to block off the sunlight. None of the lights were on, of course, so once the room was dim, I produced a fat, colorful candle from the bag Koizumi had brought, placing it on an antique candle stand and lighting it with a match. I then put some incense in a small bowl and lit it as well. Once I'd confirmed that the fragrant and strangely colored smoke was wafting around the room, I gave Nagato the sign.

Shamisen hated to be held that way, but somehow the usually grouchy cat offered no resistance as Nagato picked him up.

I coughed. "Can I ask you to put your dog next to Rousseau?"

Suspicion at what seemed like our preparations for a magic spell colored the face of the young, refined Higuchi, but she did as I asked. There were now two dogs on the sofa, each of them listless and inattentive, as though lacking in spirit.

Holding the cat, Nagato knelt down in front of the sofa.

That was the last step. I hit the switch on a digital recorder, and a haunting refrain of theremin and sitar filled the room with its eerie melody. To be honest, I thought this was overdoing it, but Koizumi's specialty was seeing his gimmicks through to the end.

The candlelight flickered uncertainly, the sweet smell of incense filled the air, and exotic music played as Nagato began what could only be thought of as a strange ritual.

"..."

In the dim room, her pale face seemed freeze-dried in its lack of affect. Her hands, just as pale as her face, moved. She placed one hand on Rousseau's head, petting him, then put that same hand to Shamisen's head. Despite being in an unfamiliar house and directly facing two strange dogs, Shamisen sat impressively still and let her do it.

Nagato brought Shamisen face-to-face with Rousseau, their noses almost touching. Rousseau's black eyes moved sluggishly to meet the eyes of the calico cat opposite him. Nagato moved her hands back and forth as if transferring something from Rousseau to Shamisen, then performed the same process with Mike. Nagato's lips were moving slightly, forming words I couldn't quite make out, but only Koizumi and I seemed to notice this.

Finally, Nagato touched Shamisen's small forehead to each dog's nose, then stood. Saying nothing, she put Shamisen back in the carrier, then brought it over to me and looked up.

"It is finished."

Naturally, everyone was dumbfounded. I certainly was, standing there holding the carrier, but Haruhi and Asahina, and especially Sakanaka and Higuchi, were all the more stunned.

Haruhi's mouth hung open. "What do you mean, 'It is finished'? That's all? I mean...what *was* that?"

"..."

Nagato merely tilted her head and directed her gaze to the two dogs, as if to say, *that's* what you should be looking at.

And there—

There were two dogs, unsteady but clear-eyed as they adorably looked about for their owners.

"Rousseau!"

"Mike!"

Sakanaka and Higuchi ran over, arms outstretched. The dogs whined weakly but wagged their tails as they licked their owners' cheeks.

A few minutes after the moving scene, which had caused Asahina to start crying out of sheer sympathy, the dingy spell-casting space had been returned to its natural living-room state. Rous-

seau and Mike were in the kitchen getting a meal from Mrs. Sakanaka, while the five of us, along with Sakanaka and Higuchi, sat on a sofa that encircled an expensive-looking table.

"What Nagato performed was a form of animal therapy." Koizumi's explanation was almost painful to listen to, but between his cheerful smile and pleasant tone, everybody seemed to be buying it. "The candle and the incense both had aromatics in them, which dogs are even more sensitive to than humans, thanks to their excellent noses. We chose the music for its relaxing qualities."

There had to be a limit to such nonsense, but I supposed all was well, since Rousseau and Mike had actually recovered. Sakanaka's and Higuchi's happiness was total, and Mrs. Sakanaka was very grateful that both her dog's and her daughter's health had been restored, and she baked a mountain of the *choux à la crème* Haruhi loved so much.

Sakanaka was even happier than her mother. "It's just incredible, Nagato! You knew stuff even the veterinarian didn't know!"

"That's our Yuki. She's the SOS Brigade's number one all-rounder," bragged Haruhi. Nagato was busy devouring *choux à la crème*. "She's read a million books, knows all kinds of things, plays the guitar, and she's a great cook too. She's even national level at sports!"

"It's a good thing that folk cure was in an old book Nagato read," said Sakanaka.

Koizumi elegantly sipped his tea, then followed that up. "There are treatments in Chinese medicine whose effectiveness science can't explain. It seems one can't dismiss folk remedies out of hand," he said. I couldn't help but think he was laying it on pretty thick.

Having served their purpose, the incense and candles were back in the bag. Shamisen, who'd likewise been used as a tool for this treatment, was in his carrier. I wanted to let him out to wander around a bit, but if he decided to sharpen his claws on any of the house's fine furniture, a simple scolding wasn't going to fix things, so I left him where he was. Ever since Nagato had stepped away, he'd been rattling around in the carrier meowing, but if I left him alone, I figured he'd give up and go to sleep.

The truth was that Shamisen was the one who deserved a medal; the other "tools" had been mere window dressing, though only Nagato, Koizumi, and I knew that little fact.

All Nagato had needed to do was freeze the data life-form element. That was all.

She could have frozen it within the two dogs that had contracted the "disease." It was the simplest and most direct method, but it could also cause problems. Higuchi's little Mike or Sakanaka's beloved Rousseau might reach the end of his natural life, but after he passed away, the frozen data life-form would remain. We couldn't ignore the possibility that it would then escape its frozen state and go on to cause more trouble. So we decided it would be better to place it in a form we could continuously monitor. Any organic life-form would suffice as a host—even Haruhi or me—but Nagato identified Shamisen as the one least likely to experience problems. This was a male calico that once in a while gained the ability to speak human language. I didn't think storing a frozen cosmic life-form or two inside him was going to cause him any difficulty, and if there *were* any problems, I would notice immediately...so that was the plan.

As an alternative to the sigh I wanted to heave, I popped a *choux à la crème* into my mouth.

While Sakanaka had certainly suffered misfortune, the source of that misfortune had now been transferred into my cat. I wondered if anyone would bother feeling sorry for me.

Nagato's apartment did allow pets, so I could leave Shamisen there with her, but convincing my sister to agree to that would take no small amount of effort, and I'd grown fond of the cat myself. You go right ahead, Shamisen. Live long enough to turn into a ghost cat yourself.

By the time we were leaving Sakanaka's house, Rousseau and Mike had gotten so much of their energy back it was unbelievable. This delighted both Asahina and Haruhi, and they each hugged both of the dogs in turn, smiling hugely.

Before we left, Mrs. Sakanaka made us take all sorts of goodies—including all the leftover *choux à la crème*. The bag thrust into Nagato's hands was especially large, and it was a good feeling to see the person who deserved the most thanks be treated so well. In the course of chatting, Higuchi (who *did* attend a ladies' college) also expressed a desire to thank us materially, but Haruhi shut her down.

"It's fine, it's fine! We took this case on for free from the beginning. Just getting to hold Mikey here is plenty. My SOS Brigade isn't a for-profit establishment anyway, and we don't need money or goods to get along. The feeling we get seeing J.J. and Mikey healthy is more than enough compensation. Right, Yuki?"

Nagato said nothing, but nodded minutely.

Always maintaining his cool, Koizumi spoke to Sakanaka. "If any other dogs fall ill in a similar manner to Rousseau, please notify us. It is unlikely, but just in case."

"I will. I'll ask around next time I take Rousseau on a walk." Sakanaka nodded firmly.

We parted ways with our classmate, saying we'd meet again at school. Haruhi started walking, her spirits high. Behind her, something occurred to me.

If Haruhi and Sakanaka happened to be in the same class next year, that would be an extremely good thing.

*   *   *

Both on the way to the station and on the train itself, Haruhi seemed to have forgotten a certain something as she happily talked about the dogs with Asahina. It would make things a lot easier for me if she didn't remember, so I was careful not to say anything foolish.

We ended up gradually going our separate ways before arriving at the station where we usually met up. Haruhi, Nagato, and Asahina all got off one stop before there, since it was closer to their homes. And though it was barely afternoon, I was already stuffed with *crème*, and I also had the cat with me, so I took a pass on going into a restaurant. So the SOS Brigade's day came to an end.

Koizumi got off at the same station as me, walking through the same turnstile.

He matched my stride, walking alongside me as I headed home. So he'd lived in this area all along, eh?

Now that the boisterous, outgoing ladies of the SOS Brigade had gone their separate ways, I walked alone with the esper, and the quiet was unnerving.

"Good work today," said Koizumi.

I couldn't help hearing that as a mere pleasantry, I said.

"Well, the source of the problem was extremely...problematic. We even had to enlist Shamisen's help. Still, Nagato certainly has been useful, hasn't she? As I recall, there was a similar problem last year. Kimidori came to us for help, and we had to save the computer club president from a data life-form. Doesn't it seem that the clients who've approached us are all connected to Nagato?"

"What're you trying to say?"

"Nagato's membership in the SOS Brigade has become a total necessity, though that's merely my opinion. I'd venture that you're the one who has more things he wants to say."

I wasn't really doing that much thinking. My only thought was to wonder why all these things—the cave cricket, the guy we'd just dealt with—kept being attracted to Earth, like a magnet attracting iron. What explained that? Come to think of it, Nagato was the same way. But Nagato was only here to watch Haruhi—

I stopped dead in my tracks.

*Haruhi.*

Was that the answer? Haruhi had created the data explosion that caused the Data Overmind to send Nagato here. But that had been an active, deliberate response. But the thing that had happened with the computer club president's room and this weird virus thing falling to Earth in a silicon lump—surely their aim wasn't Haruhi as well. The former had come to Earth millions of years ago, for one thing.

If Haruhi were unconsciously reaching back in time and manipulating things, then that meant things had well and truly gotten out of hand. But if Asahina…if time travelers had come to this time period, then that meant—

I was trying to think about it seriously when Koizumi butted in, his timing so perfect that he must've either heard me muttering to myself or wanted to deliberately interrupt my train of thought.

"Do you think it's a coincidence?" he said, repeating the unpleasant question like a waiter reading a customer's order back to him.

I felt like I knew what he was going to say. "Just spit it out. I've got no intention of playing mind games with you."

"Of all the places it could have fallen, this cosmic life-form landed here in our town and just happened to attach itself to a dog owned by a student of North High, Sakanaka, who just happened to come to the SOS Brigade for help, and we…that is to say, *Nagato* just happened to realize the truth and take action. If this is all the product of a series of coincidences, then the probability of it happening just so is astronomically tiny."

It was in my nature to want to disagree with him. It wasn't that I was on Haruhi's side.

"It was astronomical, all right! We had to intervene with two different alien-things. If it wasn't a coincidence, then what was it? Are you saying that Nagato set them up, just like you orchestrated those mysteries?"

"Surely not. If it were scripted, then it would either be the Data Overmind or some other alien of which we are yet unaware. What's certain is that this did not happen because Haruhi wished it so."

How did he know that? Wasn't it possible that she just wanted to get in one last incident before spring break came and she had too much free time on her hands? And that in thinking that, it happened? I said.

"Haven't I said it before? Suzumiya's psyche is becoming more and more stable. Almost anticlimactically so. And that's the problem."

I stayed quiet, letting him continue. Koizumi put a finger to his lips thoughtfully.

"There's something out there that finds a stable Suzumiya to be less interesting. Be it a data flare, a time-quake, or closed space, whatever the form—there's something out there that wants to provoke Suzumiya's inexplicable power into action."

Koizumi's smile was gradually changing. It was starting to look like Ryoko Asakura's.

"This incident may be only an omen of something else."

Like what? If everything were an omen, then even I could call myself a prophet and set up shop as Nostradamus II, I said.

Koizumi smirked cynically. "The timing of these extraterrestrial visits cannot be explained by coincidence. You must know. These aliens, these intelligences that hide among us—they are not limited to humanoid interfaces to the Data Overmind."

"Tch."

I didn't want to do anything dramatic, but I sneered and clicked my tongue. Koizumi sometimes seemed like he wanted to cast things in the worst possible light, but I wasn't having it. If he wanted to call Nagato a humanoid interface, fine. It was the truth.

"I'm more worried about these other aliens you're hinting at."

"The Agency has a variety of information sources, which keeps me aware of a variety of things. I can't say everything, but, well, yes." Koizumi's smile finally returned to normal mode. "I'll leave the other aliens to Nagato. My role is to work against the Agency's rival organization. I have a feeling they'll be trying something again, soon. Likewise, I'll let Asahina do something about the other faction of time travelers."

From Koizumi's expression, I could tell that he wasn't serious about that last part, but I was. The only difference was that I wasn't thinking of our Asahina; I was thinking of the older one.

No worrying was necessary in the case of Nagato. I was entirely confident that there wasn't a being anywhere whose willpower was greater than hers. And you, Koizumi—if it comes down to it, you'll be running around with me. I'll say it as many times as I have to. I won't let you forget the promise you made on that snowy mountain.

"I remember it, of course. And even if I did forget, I'm quite certain that you'd remind me. Wouldn't you?" He smiled pleasantly and gestured. "When the time comes."


"Welcome home!"

When I got back to my room, my sister was sprawled out on my bed, reading my comics.

"Hey, where'd you take Shami to?"

Not answering, I let Shamisen out of the carrier. The calico immediately jumped up onto the bed, walked onto my sister's back, and started kneading it with his paws, as though giving her a massage. She laughed, ticklish, and kicked her feet about.

"Kyon, get Shami off me! I can't get up!"

I picked up the cat, and my sister sat up. She was a fifth grader, eleven years old, but soon she'd be in the final year of elementary school. She tossed the comic book aside and started petting Shamisen like crazy, as he curled up on the bed. She sniffed at him.

"He smells sorta sweet! What is it?"

I gave her the *choux à la crème* Mrs. Sakanaka had given us. Keeping an eye on my sister as she delightedly devoured them, I picked up a hardcover book that was lying on my desk.

It had been about a week earlier. I'd borrowed it from Nagato's bookshelf as a way to cool down as final exams were wrapping up. "Got any good books that might fit my mood?" I'd asked Nagato, and after standing stiffly in front of her bookshelf for about five minutes, she'd slowly thrust this at me. I'd only gotten halfway through it, but it was just the story of a romance between a boy and girl as they go from high school to college, with no SF or mystery or fantasy elements, just an ordinary world—and in many ways, both then and now, it suited me just fine. When she grew up, Nagato shouldn't go into aromatherapy or fortune-telling or veterinary work—she should be a librarian.

I flopped down on the bed and started reading as my sister went to the kitchen to look for something to drink, holding her second *crème* in hand.

I wonder how much time passed.

I'd been absorbed in the book, and when I came to, Shamisen was scratching at the door, which was his way of telling me he wanted me to open it and let him out. I normally leave it half open so he can come and go as he pleases, but my sister had closed it when she'd left.

Sticking a bookmark in the book, I opened the door for the cat. Shamisen slunk out into the hallway, pausing to turn and *meow* at me by way of thanks. But then he kept looking, staring at something behind me. I followed his gaze and looked back.

It was the corner of the ceiling. There was nothing. Nothing was there.

Shamisen's wide-eyed gaze at the ceiling's corner began, slowly, to move. The object of his stare was now the exterior wall. It was as though something invisible had been on the ceiling, but had slid across and down the wall.

"Hey."

But Shamisen was only thus occupied for a few seconds. The only part of him that heard my call was the tip of his tail. I heard his quiet footfalls recede as he headed away, perhaps down to the kitchen after my sister to see if he could arrange for some dinner.

I closed the door most of the way but left it open wide enough so that the cat could get back in, and I thought about what I'd just seen. Shamisen's actions weren't especially rare. Animals often reacted to small movements that humans ignored, their ears pricking at minute sounds coming in from outside.

But. What if.

What if there had been something there, invisible to humans, that Shamisen could see. What if that invisible whatever-it-was had been stuck to my ceiling, then crawled over and down my wall. What then?

—*Do souls exist?*

—*That is classified.*

What if millions, or tens of millions of years ago, data life-forms had fallen to Earth and chose not dogs as their hosts, but humans? Was there a non-zero possibility that a human would not fall ill as Rousseau had, but instead would coexist with it? Was it too much of a leap to wonder if that was the source of early humans' great leap in intelligence?

If that were so, then perhaps the organic life-forms that so intrigued Nagato's boss could begin to amass knowledge. Not on their own, but with the unwitting help of extraterrestrials.

It would've been very strange if I'd figured something out that the Data Overmind had overlooked, but just as mitochondria had once been independent organisms, what if these spiritual symbionts had improved the mental capacity of ancient apes, and had been passed down through to present day? The logic made sense—

"Sure, whatever."

It was totally unlike me to be thinking about this stuff. Humans couldn't imagine stuff that was beyond their own abilities, after all. Especially not me. I'd leave pondering difficult problems to Koizumi. Just like he left dealing with aliens to Nagato, I'd stay in the listener's position when it came to this stuff. I understood, too, the nature of the condescending promise he'd made. *If it comes to that, I may switch sides*, he'd said. *Consider it a warning.* The many times he'd said such things seemed like nothing more than him carefully building an alibi.

Sorry, Koizumi, but alibis are doomed to be destroyed. Cheap, shallow excuses aren't gonna fly with me. Or with Haruhi.

And anyway. Even if Koizumi's ability to move was ended by whatever intrigues the Agency got up to, I still had other options. If nothing else, I could prostrate myself before the all-knowing, all-powerful Tsuruya. If that brilliant, cheerful upperclassman devoted her grinning shrewdness to covert maneuvering, even the Agency's top brass would be in real trouble.

How I would do such things, or having done such things, what would happen—I hadn't devoted so much as a millisecond of brain power to that. I'd worry about that later.

"...Worrying about those things really isn't my specialty."

But whatever. I couldn't be anybody besides myself, and my consciousness was mine alone. Mine! All mine!

And if somebody wanted it back, well, tough—the statute of limitations had long since passed on that one.

As I was pondering such pointless nonsense, my cell phone, which I'd left on my desk, began to vibrate. I picked it up, wondering if the call was going to be delivering some kind of future warning—but it was just Haruhi.

"What's up?"

"Hey, Kyon. I forgot something important," said Haruhi, getting right to the point of her phone call without any preamble. "It's great that we cured J.J. and Mike, but why do you think they caught that weird sickness in the first place? What I think is that the two of them really *did* see a ghost, and the shock made them sick!"

See, Koizumi? Do you see why I was worrying about the post-incident cleanup? It's because she thinks about stuff like this.

"I bet it was there on that path we walked until about a week ago. My guess is that it still hasn't cut its ties with the mortal world. It's probably turned into a wandering spirit, just going all over the place!"

"I don't know anything about ghosts, but you should just let it go to Heaven already."

"That's why we're having an all-hands meeting tomorrow! This time we're *definitely* gonna get a picture with that ghost."

"And just how are you gonna line up with a ghost, huh?"

"We can't do it during the day, I bet. We'll do it at night. We'll find a place where ghosts probably congregate, and we'll take a bunch of pictures. They'll have to show up on at least one or two of 'em, right?"

Haruhi unilaterally informed me of the meeting time and hung up before bothering to ask if I had plans on Sunday. I had no doubt that seconds later, she was contacting the other brigade members. Apparently tomorrow's mysterious phenomena patrol would take the form of searching for haunted spots in the dead of night.

I put my phone down and gazed again at the corner of my room.

Sakanaka's ghost problem had, via her dog's illness, ended up in Nagato's jurisdiction. I knew very well that a ghost hadn't been involved at all, as did Koizumi. But the notion had evidently lingered in Haruhi's head, such that a few hours later, she remembered it. Our esteemed brigade chief was now hoping not for alien whatever-based life-forms from space, but bona fide ghosts.

In any case, I'd entrust Koizumi with the job of putting marks on the city map. If we actually managed to take a real spectral photograph, I'd let him come up with a pseudo-scientific excuse too. I planned to take on the weighty job of walking through the night air with Asahina, letting her cling to me at every little noise.

Our bizarre brigade, walking all over creation snapping pictures in the dark. Any outsider would think *we* were the strange ones, wandering around trying to take pictures of invisible ghosts. Nevertheless, the weather would soon be turning warmer, and we could probably explain away our behavior by citing spring fever. In the worst-case scenario, we could always get Asahina to dress up as a shrine maiden and chant the Heart Sutra. It'd be an exorcism Haruhi-style.

Even if ghosts did exist, I doubted they would be swarming around such that you could run into them just by walking around. It wasn't like Haruhi actually wanted to meet one.

Having watched her for close to a year, I was sure of that much. What she liked best was not ghosts, but the action of searching for ghosts with her friends.

And for my part, well—

"I guess I wouldn't mind if one showed up," I muttered to the place on the ceiling where Shamisen had looked, then went back to reading my book. The reality portrayed in that book was far more ordinary than the one that surrounded me.

But that didn't mean I was jealous of the more realistic reality.

Not now, anyway.

# AFTERWORD

**About books.**

The other day, for no particular reason, I hauled a cardboard box out of the back of my closet. Inside were all the books I'd bought and read when I was younger.

Incidentally, I tend to be quite a packrat, and I'll keep stuff around unless it's obviously garbage. Fortunately, I'm also someone who thinks really hard before buying anything, so the number of boxes around my house stays manageable, but when my eyes alight on the cover of a book I haven't seen in a decade, it's enough to make me want to say, "Argh, how dare you!"

And when I really thought about it, it occurred to me that the collected memories of reading all these books must have really shaped my thinking patterns. Of course, it's not like I remembered every little detail of every book, but it's definitely true that some of those memories did not evaporate, but rather sank into my mind where they quiver even now.

What impressed me most of all, and what is indeed a very important point, is the idea of timing. The fact that I read certain books when I did is what allowed them to leave such a deep impression on me; if I were to read them for the first time now, the impression would be quite different.

You could say that the sum of all the writing I read in the past is the distant ancestor to the writing I do now—and the writing I'll do in the future. It might be the case that if I'd missed even one of those books, you might not even be reading this afterword.

So it was that I closed up the cardboard box with a feeling of deep gratitude, putting it back in the closet as I promised myself I would reread every one of those books someday, hoping that the new writing I read in the future will likewise become elements of my future self.

## About cats.

I get cold very easily, and I sometimes wonder if I wear a winter jacket more days out of the year than anyone else in the world. People tease me about it all the time, and all I can think to do is answer, "Maybe I was a cat in a former life." The truth or falsity of reincarnation aside, if I am a reincarnated cat, then that cat also had its own former life—and if in its former life it had been a polar bear, would the cat prefer warm weather or cold? And what about if that cat were then reincarnated as a penguin? Or is reincarnation specific to humans? There was that TV show with the person who did pet fortune-telling based on the pets' past lives, so I figure if they can do it, I can do it. I spent an entire day thinking about it.

## About "Editor in Chief, Full Speed Ahead!"

I've been wondering since the beginning what would happen if the SOS Brigade had to do some kind of activity as the literature club. Quite some time ago, I wrote down a short note that said "literary anthology/literature club activities" along with an untitled short piece about Yuki Nagato, but while I remember writing it, I have no idea where on my hard drive it might be, and finding it would be a pain.

Other notes I jotted down around the same time include "the student council finally makes its move," "counseling/computer club/shut-in," "Haruhi's disappearance," and "baseball tournament." It all seems so nostalgic now. There were many others, but they're either spoilers or meaningless details, so I reluctantly omitted them, then spent the rest of the day clicking my way through the ocean of data looking for other fragments. Can I get someone else to do my searching for me, I wonder?

## About "Wandering Shadow"

I always agonize over book titles and even chapter titles, and when I get really desperate I'll just write some random English word. In this case, I translated the temporary title that had just hit me—"*samayou kage*"—into English. No desperation required!

Come to think of it, I didn't think about the title *The Melancholy of Haruhi Suzumiya* much at all. I'm pretty sure it took me about ten seconds to decide on it. I couldn't think of anything better. I always start writing before I think of a title and only add the title once I'm done, but because I have accepted the reality of my unfortunate lack of copywriting sense, I'm always very slapdash about it. Maybe somebody else should do this for me. Please?

Thus it is that this suddenly strangely titled series has come to the conclusion of its eighth volume. This is thanks to the many professionals involved in the publication and circulation of the book, in addition to the readers who so kindly pick it up. Thank you so much. My thanks also goes to the many people who've supported this title in media other than prose. I shall see you again.

Farewell.